Angel in Waiting

by

Sharon Saracino

The Earthbound Series, Volume 3

Angel in Waiting

Cover Art by *Debbie Taylor*

The Wild Rose Press, Inc.
PO Box 708
Adams Basin, NY 14410-0708
Visit us at www.thewildrosepress.com

Publishing History
First Fantasy Rose Edition, 2015
Print ISBN 978-1-62830-879-2
Digital ISBN 978-1-62830-880-8

The Earthbound Series, Volume 3
Published in the United States of America

Taking a deep breath,
Dimitri carefully lowered his arm and rested his hand on her nearly naked hip. Gritting his teeth against the silky texture of her skin, he pulled her into him. She sighed softly, and his heart twisted, battling a war between contentment and consternation. Elle Gates was human, fragile, doomed, her limited lifetime a blip on the radar of his long existence. Nothing but pain awaited him. And hell, considering she was human, there were no guarantees the bond had any effect on her at all. This attraction could be all one sided. Still, in this time, at this moment, he couldn't deny it. Holding her in his arms and thinking of her as his felt…right.

Mac's wife had put her faith in Dimitri to keep her friend safe, and he fully intended to do so. Even if he couldn't quite decide whether his determination to protect her stemmed from his promise to Kat or his own desire. It was irrelevant at the moment. Something had this woman spooked enough to run from a successful career, everything and everyone she knew and loved, without a word. As the first faint fingers of dawn stole through the gap in the drapes and inched across the room toward the bed, Dimitri reluctantly disentangled himself from Elle's arms and gathered up his things. With a lingering look at her peaceful face, he faded from the room with plenty of questions but absolutely no answers.

Praise for Sharon Saracino

"Sharon Saracino's world of angels, archangels, witches, demons, and evil minions engages the reader from page one. Make no plans for your weekend—you won't be able to put down any of these stories."

~*Sharon Buchbinder, Author, Obsession*

Dedication

To my readers...you are all rock stars and I thank you
from the bottom of my heart for all of your support!
~*~
And as always, to my Vince,
who makes everything I do possible.

Chapter One

Trapped in the darkest recesses of her mind, Elle Gates floundered in desperation, a prisoner in a circus of madness, imprisoned in the suffocating darkness of a dream that squeezed her heart and sucked at her soul. Scenes and sounds broke apart all around her and reconfigured like jagged pieces of glass scattered by an unseen hand across the vast nothingness of this smothering reality. Each piece reflected a strange face, a new horror. Her senses screamed as her body snagged on the sharp edged splinters of empty eyes and souls twisted in torment, leaving her cut and bleeding. And she was cold. As cold as death.

Trying to scream with a tongue knotted in fear, Elle watched helplessly as a glinting dagger whistled through the air, straight at her heart. The searing pain woke her, as sharp and real as the moment the blade had actually penetrated her flesh. She pressed a hand to her chest and found it damp. Though the wound was well healed, her skin remained moist with remembered terror.

The nightmare rarely varied and still she couldn't separate her own memories from those of the demon who had possessed her. At least her father and his associates hadn't made an appearance in the convoluted horrors tonight. For a moment she lay staring into the darkness, the pounding of her heart and her ragged breathing the only sounds disturbing the stillness. Her pulse slowly resumed a normal rhythm once she wakened and realized the demon was truly gone and she was free. Physically, at least. Some nights she wondered if her mind would ever truly belong to her again.

"What time is it?" she croaked. Though not a twitch of movement or a whisper of sound gave his presence away, she knew he was there. He was always there when she woke from the nightmares. Dimitri Radchenko, the *Earthbound* angel who'd been given the unenviable task of her care following the fiasco in Rome. Thanks to his medical skills and supernatural powers, Elle survived what she knew should have been a fatal injury.

Hot tears gathered beneath her lids. Elle could hardly blame her best friend's husband, Kassian McAllister, for banishing her to the States with a complete stranger. After all, Elle had foolishly unleashed a demon, wreaked havoc across two continents, and buried Kassian's sister, Callista McAllister, alive. Oh, yeah. Good times.

"Nearly seven. You slept almost six hours this time before the nightmare hit."

"Well, isn't that special? Yay, me," Elle muttered, untangling her bare legs from the damp sheets. She slid from the bed, tugging the hem of her nightshirt down over her thighs. Waking up to a hulking, leather-clad giant in one's room, night after night, should be unnerving. However, after the initial shock wore off, Elle came to depend on his quiet presence as an anchor to reality when she awoke in a state of panic.

As soon as she was well enough, she'd insisted on

moving out of the McAllister's New York penthouse, where Dimitri had originally taken her, and back to her own modest condo. That had been over three weeks ago. She'd expected it would be the end of her association with Dimitri. Yet, every time she woke from the nightmare in the dead of night, he was there. Waiting. Watching. She was grateful. Not that she was about to admit it. And she sure as hell wouldn't attempt to explain it. Not even to herself.

"I made coffee." The familiar creak of wood and leather in the darkness indicated Dimitri had risen from the small chair, which struggled to accommodate his massive size.

"Of course you did. You're going to make somebody a great wife someday, Dimitri."

Dimitri grunted in response. A triangular sliver of light pierced the darkened room as he opened the door into the hallway. Once he closed the door behind him, Elle clicked on the lamp and frowned. Her bed resembled a battlefield. She tried tugging the bedclothes into a semblance of order, then gave up with a resigned sigh, and headed for the bathroom.

Ten minutes and gallons of hot water later, Elle felt almost human. After toweling off quickly, she tugged on a pair of comfortable jeans faded to a perfect blue and a simple black tee. Shunning make-up, she slicked her wet hair into a high ponytail. Following the scent of Columbian dark roast to her sleek, modern kitchen, she found Dimitri already perched at the breakfast bar with two steaming mugs, an open box of doughnuts, and the morning paper spread out in front of him.

He looked up as she entered and slid a mug across the dark granite counter in her direction.

"Thanks." Elle perched a barstool away and took a large, healthy sip. He nudged the box in her direction, and she shook her head with a tired smile.

"I'll pass. Maybe a guy your size can put away a dozen of those things a day, but just looking at them packs five pounds on my hips. I have to leave this apartment sometime. Since I can't just dematerialize like you *Earthbound* guys do, I'll still need to fit through the door."

She pulled her cell phone across the counter and checked the display. Her agent had been ringing her phone off the hook, but Elle had nothing to say. All of her contractual obligations were met, and she hadn't written a word since she'd sent off her last manuscript before the world crashed down around her. Dancing with a demon had sucked her soul dry of hearts, flowers, and happy-ever-afters.

That was bad enough, but the note that arrived yesterday was an even bigger game changer. While in possession of her body and her mind, the demon Azakriel had apparently found it necessary to contact her bastard father and share her whereabouts. She knew it was only a matter of time before he or one of his cronies came knocking on the door. Her freedom, and quite possibly her life, would be forfeit. After all these years, she'd dared to believe she could forget, could put it all behind her and live life as Elle Gates forever. A life made possible only by Kat's generous nature in taking her at face value all those years ago. Deceit was a hell of a way to repay an unconditional friendship. But facts were facts, and apparently, you couldn't escape them, no matter how fast you ran or how cleverly you thought you'd concealed them. If her father came calling, not only would the monstrous truth of her origins be revealed, her lies would be exposed, and everyone she cared about would be at risk simply by association. It was time to go.

"Your hips look fine to me." Dimitri's dark eyes regarded her over the rim of his coffee cup, briefly flicking up and down, before glancing away. "In fact, if anything, you've lost weight."

"Ah, the magic words every woman lives to hear," Elle forcibly dragged her thoughts back to the present, batted her lashes and smiled, giving in to temptation and snagging a chocolate glazed. "So what's on your agenda for the day?"

"Depends. What's on yours?"

"Well," Elle chewed thoughtfully, swallowed a bite of doughnut, and washed it down with a sip of coffee. "Suppose I said I planned to clean the bathroom and then curl up with a good book?"

"In that case, I'd say I'm heading uptown to meet with Mac and then crashing at my place for a couple of hours of uninterrupted sleep. I'd also say I'm suffering from a serious case of déjà vu since I'm pretty sure you've said the same damn thing every day this week. How much cleaning can a twenty-five square foot bathroom used by one small woman require?"

"Cleanliness is next to godliness, Big Guy. McAllister, huh? So, I guess they're back." Elle slid from the stool and moved stiffly around the breakfast bar. Rinsing a sponge in the black farmhouse sink, she turned her back to him, and began furiously scrubbing the already spotless counters.

"Well, in that case, you're a shoe-in for sainthood. You have to deal with Kat sometime, you know."

Dimitri reached around her to snag the coffeepot and refill his cup. She hadn't even heard him move. For a man who was the size of a mountain, he moved with the stealth and grace of a jungle cat. Elle gripped the sponge so hard she risked tearing it in half. Thinking Dimitri had returned to his seat, she spun around and gasped as she found herself staring at a broad, muscular chest straining the confines of his black tee. She stepped back automatically, but there was nowhere to go. Trapped between him and the counter, she tilted her head back to look at him.

"Not yet." She dropped her eyes, unable to hold his gaze. Once she was gone, it wouldn't matter anymore. Better she disappear and allow Kat and the others to believe she was a coward too ashamed to face them after her idiocy, than stick around and cause more pain.

A thick, calloused finger caught her under the chin and forced her eyes up. Her mouth went dry. Dimitri Radchenko with his long hair, dark eyes, and high Slavic cheekbones looked like a biker who'd gotten on the wrong side of a bar fight. His long, straight nose shadowed a pair of full, well-formed lips that had a tendency to twist into a grimace at a moment's notice. They were twisted now. The expression accentuated the wicked scar running along the right side of his face from his temple to the corner of his mouth, disguised somewhat by the thin line of neatly-manicured beard shadowing his jaw and upper lip. His appearance alone probably scared the living hell out of most people. But Elle had never been most people, and far from being intimidated by him, she found him uncomfortably appealing. Even now, though they barely touched, she imagined she felt his heat penetrating her clothes.

6

Breathing deeply, she filled her lungs with the comfortable leather scent of him, pleasantly mingled with soap and herbal shampoo. Her pulse hitched, her breath quickened. Menacing or not, he incited a riot of feelings she didn't want to examine too closely. One look into those deep brown eyes surrounded by long, dark lashes that had a tendency to tangle, and she didn't see an edgy bad boy. She saw right into his soul. A soul crying out to hers.

"Shit!" His hand dropped away as though he'd been burned. He turned on his heel and stomped back to his barstool, placing the counter between them. Elle quickly shuttered her mind. Dimitri was an *Earthbound*, an order of angels cast from the heavens for sedition as *Fallen* millennia ago. A select few redeemed their souls by arbitrating an agreement to forfeit their wings and dedicate themselves to battling the evil ones on Earth. Like all *Earthbound*, Dimitri Radchenko could read the thoughts of anyone around him unless they knew how to block him. Elle learned to shield her mind years ago. Unfortunately, lately, she was so preoccupied she didn't always remember to do so. Judging by his dark flush and darker expression, she'd been broadcasting loud and clear, and Dimitri didn't agree with her assessment of his character.

"Don't worry, Radchenko. Your secret's safe with me."

"I have no idea what you're talking about."

"I wouldn't dream of besmirching your reputation. The fact that your *Fallen* slaying, bike riding, knife wielding, leather-clad ass is nothing but a front hiding a heart too big for your own good will stay just between us, m'kay?"

"You obviously have me confused with one of the characters from your books. I'm nobody's hero, so don't start thinking I am. And stop trying to change the subject. No one blames you for what happened except you. Kat sure as hell doesn't, and according to Mac, she's making herself sick with worry. If you really cared for her as much as you claim, you'd put her out of her misery and talk to her."

"I buried McAllister's sister alive, Dimitri. I tried to kill her. I hurt people I love, and God knows what else I may have done between the time I left Kat's house in Pennsylvania and the time I arrived in Rome. What the hell am I supposed to say? Oopsie?" Elle had no real recollection of the days when the demon had inhabited her body—the particular demon she'd been naive enough to unleash used people's hidden desires to obliterate the filter between right and wrong. She knew what happened in Rome only because she'd been told. Elle's case of temporary lust for Kat's brother, Luca, had almost cost Callista McAllister her life.

"You aren't responsible for your actions while under the influence of a demon."

"But I'm the one who set him free." Elle threw the sponge into the sink where it landed with a sad, wet plop. Going through Kat's things and opening the book had been stupid and careless and self-serving. It was only right it should cost her something. But did it have to cost her everything?

"That was an accident," Dimitri tipped back his mug and polished off his second cup.

"Yeah, *that* was an accident." She hadn't been looking to free a demon. She'd simply been trying to free herself. She blew out a long, slow breath. "Well, thanks for the coffee. Again. I'm not planning to leave the house, but honestly, Dimitri, I'm a big girl. If I do decide to go out, I don't need a babysitter."

"Didn't say you did. But you're fairly well known, and for all intents and purposes, you've gone from being someone who's always been very visible to someone who hasn't been seen in weeks. People are curious. Photographers are staking out the place. You might need someone to run interference." He stood and stretched his arms over his head until his back audibly cracked. Elle lowered her eyes quickly when she realized he'd caught her staring at the rippling play of muscle under his tee. "You know how to get a hold of me if you need me."

"Thanks, but I won't."

"Okay, see ya." He departed with the same phrase every day, as though they might meet again, or they might not. Yet, every night he returned and parked himself in that chair, her reluctant Guardian Angel.

"Yep, see ya," Elle replied with a casual wave. She refused to analyze the funny little pang twisting in her chest knowing it was a lie. When Dimitri returned tonight to watch over her, she would be long gone.

"What?" she asked when she realized Dimitri was still standing there regarding her with a puzzled expression and narrowed eyes. He didn't answer, simply shook his head and disappeared.

The condo felt curiously empty when he'd left. She'd grown accustomed to having the big lug around, like a favorite robe or a comfortable pair of slippers. Or something. She realized with a sinking feeling that she would miss him. If only she'd come clean earlier. From the very beginning. Now the damage was done, and she couldn't un-ring the bell. If her father showed up and the truth came out, Kat would never forgive her. None of them would.

Chapter Two

Dimitri materialized in the parking garage under Elle Gates' building where his bike waited, gleaming in the artificial light. The woman was hiding something. He knew it as surely as he knew his own name, but he had yet to put his finger on it. In sleep she was an open book, but the nightmares were so convoluted it was impossible to differentiate thoughts from memories, memories from fears. Once awake, she was always on guard. Well, except for an occasional slip like she'd had this morning. Was she blind? He scared the hell out of most women, most men, too. And that was exactly the way he liked it. Easier to keep his priorities in order. Elle Gates thought he was compassionate and tender? Some kind-hearted savior? Damn demon must have screwed with her mind more than any of them suspected. Either that or she had perfected rationalization to an art form.

He'd just swung his leg over the bike when he felt it. Pinpricks of electricity raced up and down his spine, heralding the presence of evil. He carefully eased away from the bike, unsnapping his sleeves to expose the intricate tattoos on his forearms and avail himself of the weapons hidden within. Gripping a stiletto in each fist, he froze with his back to the wall and peered into the shadows of the darkened structure, eyes narrowed and focused, ears attuned to the slightest sound. A soft scuffle of a shoe, the shift of a slightly darker shadow, and Dimitri faded in a heartbeat to the far side of the garage behind a battered sedan that looked as though it hadn't moved in years.

He pinned one *animorti* to the wall with a knife at his throat and hoisted the other helplessly in the air by his neck before either of them had time to register that he'd moved. Looking from one to the other, Dimitri twisted the knife, his lips stretching in a cold grin as the bastard against the wall exploded into a puddle of slimy, black goo, and then he turned his attention back to the other, shaking his head in disgust. The *Fallen* were becoming less and less particular about their recruits. This one was little more than a kid. Of course, to the evil ones, everyone was fair game and everyone was expendable. He didn't like the idea of killing him, but the kid was already doomed and putting an end to his existence was probably the greatest kindness Dimitri could do him. The scrawny puppet stared in horrified fascination at the oily mess that had been his partner seconds earlier. Then he flicked his gaze back to Dimitri. His eyes widened and rolled back until only the whites showed, and he began to struggle in earnest. He writhed and twitched, panting in short, terrified gasps, before switching to wild kicks and punches, connecting with nothing since he still dangled a good twelve inches above the concrete. Dimitri sighed and simply waited for him to wear himself out.

It took nearly ten minutes for the *animorti* to admit defeat. Finally, when he hung limp and exhausted in Dimitri's fist, Dimitri lowered his arm until the kid's feet touched the floor, released the shirt, and flexed his aching fingers.

"How did you find me here?" He growled in a low menacing voice. The answer slapped him in the back of the head almost as soon as he asked the question. Instead of fading to Elle's as he usually did when he was through hunting for the night, he'd gotten cocky and brought the bike thinking maybe he could coax her out of the house with the offer of a ride. Yeah, as if that would interest someone like Elle. Lack of sleep must be softening his brain. He led the bastards right to her front door. Thankfully, he'd gotten to them before they'd gotten to her. If anything happened to her because of his carelessness, he'd...well, he didn't know what he'd do exactly, but it was irrelevant, anyway. He'd have the threat neutralized in just a minute.

"Well?"

The *animorti* remained stubbornly silent. Dimitri flipped the knife in the air. He caught it deftly and plunged it into the kid's chest all in one smooth and too familiar motion. As usual, Dimitri spared a thought for the family who waited and worried and would never come close to imagining what had become of the boy. What a damn waste.

"Not..." The kid gasped as his head snapped up just before he disintegrated.

"Oh, sure. Now you wanna talk," Dimitri grumbled as he slapped his stiletto against his forearm where it disappeared into his tattoo. He rubbed his palms together briskly and aimed them, and the resultant blue light, at the two puddles of remains, vaporizing them instantly. Stalking back across the garage, he threw a leg over the bike, and slammed a boot down on the kick starter.

The bike roared beneath him as he revved the

throttle and exited the garage, cruising the dawn lightened streets on his way uptown. He absorbed and embraced the power of the engine vibrating from the soles of his boots up through the muscles of his thighs. His hair hung loose and streamed behind him in a wind-whipped frenzy. This was where he belonged, alone in the shadows, ass glued to a rocket of steel and chrome, barreling down dark streets or running a blade through the *Fallen* and their *animorti* scum in some back alley or parking garage. There was no place for him in the velvet darkness and soft lamplight of satin sheets scented with sandalwood and roses. He had no business being mesmerized by the soft breasts and silky tangled limbs of a woman he could never have. A *human* woman. But he parked his ass in that chair every night watching and waiting until she woke up. Because it was his duty to figure out her secret and report it to McAllister, right? That must be it. Yeah, right.

****

"What could she possibly have to hide? It's not like there's a lot occupying that head of hers beyond the latest shoe sale."

"No clue," Dimitri replied. "But I plan to figure it out. And just for the record, you're wrong about her. There's more to the woman than meets the eye."

"Thank you, Dimitri. I've been telling him the same thing for months." Katrina McAllister strode into the room carrying a tray of coffee and Italian pastries. She set it on the cocktail table in the middle of the furniture grouping, snagged a mug for herself, and then tossed her long, silvery hair over her shoulders before curling up like a kitten on the sofa next to her husband. "You just don't know Elle like I do."

"So you keep saying, baby, but I still say there's nothing in her head but hamsters on a wheel." McAllister leaned forward to grab a mug and pluck a *cornetto* from the box indicating with a wave that Dimitri should help himself. Then he sat back and shifted his position, gluing himself to his wife from shoulder to knee. Dimitri envied them their closeness. They were bound soul mates, two halves of whole. It was something all *Earthbound* hoped for, but not all were lucky enough to find. "And I don't mean to imply Elle isn't a bright woman, or that she doesn't have redeeming qualities. I just think what you see is what you get. Not a whole lot of depth."

"I'll admit, I had the same impression at first, but there's a lot more going on in that head of hers than you give her credit for."

In fact, he'd learned the real Elle Gates couldn't be more different from the shallow, giddy, *fashionista* he'd originally thought her. Except for the same inexplicable addiction to shoes, the woman he'd come to know didn't resemble her public image in the least, and though she certainly read the romance genre she also wrote, he most often glimpsed the classics or thick volumes of non-fiction on her nightstand. In private, she dressed casually, wore her long, dark hair loose or in a messy ponytail, and was intelligent and thoughtful. In fact, he was beginning to think she was damn near perfect, and that couldn't be good. Dimitri bit into a crisp *sfogliatelle* pastry and chewed contentedly. It was nearly as good as the ones he'd gotten hooked on in Italy, and it definitely beat the sugary doughnuts he'd eaten for breakfast. He made a mental note to ask Katrina where she got them.

"There's definitely something going on with her. I'm just not sure what it is yet."

"Well, whatever it is, and for reasons I can't quite fathom, my wife loves her." Mac frowned. "Association with us is what got her into this mess, so she's our responsibility. We take care of our own."

"How is she, really?" Kat asked in a quiet voice.

"Physically, she's fine." Dimitri polished off one pastry and reached for another. "Healed a lot more quickly than I would have expected considering Luca's blade was Heaven forged and she's a human. But the nightmares? Yeah, they still drop in to say hello every night."

"Maybe she did so well because you're a hell of a doctor, brother." McAllister grinned. "Don't know why you ever stopped practicing."

"Aw hell, getting a medical degree was just something I did to kill time when *Fallen* activity was slow," Dimitri retorted. "Never took it very seriously."

In reality, he'd taken it far *too* seriously. He'd served as a medic in countless wars and political conflicts over the centuries before finally taking the time to obtain an actual college degree and license to practice. But the chaos of a battlefield wasn't quite the same as the very public arena of a busy city hospital. It wasn't long before he found it impossible to stand by helplessly and watch as lives were lost when he had the power to save them. But saving them would have revealed his true nature. Rather than sit on his thumbs and look the other way while one more needless tragedy came through his Emergency Department, he walked away. Humans were too damned fragile.

Katrina McAllister eyed him steadily over the rim

16

of her coffee cup. He met her knowing gaze and looked away with a frown. Damn pain in the ass having an empath around. Blocking his thoughts was second nature. Blocking his emotions? Yeah, not so much. Then he brightened. He was willing to bet Mac couldn't get away with a damn thing anymore.

"Well, that's it," Kat announced, unfolding her long legs from under her and jumping to her feet. "I'm going to see her whether she wants me to or not."

"And what if she won't let you in?" McAllister quirked an amused brow at his wife.

"*Earthbound* don't let a little thing like a locked door stand in their way," Kat announced, planting her fists on her denim clad hips like a silvery superhero.

"*We* don't. But *you*, my love, have yet to master the fine art of consistently fading on demand," her husband laughed, referring to the *Earthbound* ability to dematerialize and travel limited distances at will. Katrina hadn't discovered her true heritage until meeting her husband and brother, and unlike typical *Earthbounds*, hadn't spent a lifetime perfecting the skill.

"Well, I can do it *most* of the time." Her shoulders slumped and her lower lip protruded in a frustrated pout. She dropped back onto the sofa like a stone.

"I'm not telling you what to do, you understand?" Dimitri pointed the last bite of his third *sfogliatelle* in Kat's direction before popping it in his mouth. "My opinion? You should wait. She's struggling with something right now. Maybe it's guilt, maybe it's something else altogether. I don't know. But I do know she misses you, Kat. I see it on her face every time your name comes up. I think maybe she just needs more time."

Kat's large, gray eyes shimmered with tears.

"For years, each of us was all the other one had. We were family. She always stood by me and never treated me like a freak, even when it probably cost her other friends. She accepted my weird abilities without batting an eye. I want to give her the time she needs, but I can't let her think I've abandoned her."

"Seriously, Kat?" McAllister wrapped an arm around his wife and hitched her into his side with a smirk. "You think the hundreds of phone calls and text messages and almost daily flower arrangements indicate you've abandoned her? Shit, I'm considering buying the florist. It'd be cheaper in the long run."

"It's not the same thing as being there." Kat thumped her fist on her husband's broad chest and then settled into him with a sigh. Just then, McAllister's cell phone buzzed on the table beside him.

"McAllister," he barked into the device. "What? Shit! Kat, turn the television on…channel 3." He turned to Dimitri. "That was my assistant. Apparently Elle has decided to come out of seclusion. She's holding a press conference on the midday news." He tossed the phone back onto the table and sat forward as the sixty-inch screen lit up and filled the living room with a larger than life image of Elle Gates' smiling face.

Dimitri watched in stunned disbelief as a stylish, sassy, redhead in a pixie-cut looking nothing like the drawn, frail brunette he'd left standing in her kitchen this morning smiled into the camera and announced she was taking a sabbatical from her career. A sabbatical of indeterminate length. She planned to travel, she said, in order to recharge her batteries and feed her muse. Gone were the jeans and T-shirt she'd been wearing earlier, replaced by some sparkly, blue thing that caught the light and reflected into the camera as she fidgeted on a makeshift platform at the entrance to her building, nodding and smiling at the small knot of reporters scribbling down her every word. She stepped away from the microphone after thanking her agent, her editor, McAllister Publishing, and most especially her loyal readers. Frustrated shouts followed her retreating back as she hopped down from the platform and disappeared back into the building after declining to answer questions.

"What in the hell was that all about?" McAllister barked.

"She looks so thin," Kat frowned at her husband. "What are you so upset about, McAllister? So she's taking a break. It's not like you need the revenue she generates."

"I could give two shits about the money, Kat. I'm thinking of selling the company anyway. I've become a little more visible than I like. I'm just trying to figure out what's going on in her head. Elle Gates loves to write. She's a writing machine. Why would she give it up and walk away?"

"It could be my fault," Dimitri mumbled.

"Huh?" McAllister reached for the remote and clicked off the news that had moved on to coverage of a house fire in Jersey City.

"She told me she was staying in today. No big surprise there since she's only been outside to move from your place to hers since we got back from Europe. I told her to call if she decided to go out. I may have let it slip there were photographers hanging around and she might need someone to run interference."

"So, she thinks it over, makes an appearance, and announces she's taking a sabbatical…all's well, nothing to see here, folks. Bye-bye public curiosity, bye-bye creepy photographers. It's rather clever, really." Kat's grin widened. "See, Kassian. I told you she had more brains than you give her credit for. You may reward me for my brilliance later."

McAllister simply grunted as his wife planted a triumphant kiss on his jaw. Dimitri kept his own thoughts closely guarded and his expression neutral, but he knew he must have been throwing off negativity like a sanitation worker chucking trash bags into a dumpster.

"What's wrong with you?" Kat demanded. "This is a good thing, right? It's so…unexpected, so impulsive, so smart. Well, it's so Elle! Maybe she's finally coming around."

"Maybe," Dimitri agreed automatically, but he was far from convinced. Katrina McAllister might know Elle Gates better than anyone, but she knew the woman she'd been before she'd gotten up close and personal with a demon. Something like that had a tendency to change a person. He was the one who'd been with Elle almost day and night since. He was the one who'd shared Elle's nightmares and watched her struggle alone with some unidentified burden. And he was the one who suddenly had the epiphany about what had prompted the unexpected public appearance of the blue-eyed redhead with the pixie-cut and the over-bright smile. Elle Gates wasn't preparing to pick up the pieces of her life. She was preparing to run away from it.

"Gotta go." Dimitri jumped to his feet, almost

knocking the cocktail table over in his haste.

"What the hell?" McAllister groused, reaching out and grabbing the table to steady it as the remaining coffee and pastries slid to the edge and threatened to tumble to the floor. "What's your problem?"

"No problem," Dimitri stuttered, deliberately avoiding Katrina McAllister's perceptive gaze. "I just remembered I was supposed to take the bike in for service an hour ago."

A bead of sweat trickled down the back of his neck, and his heart pounded like an iron fist trying to punch its way out of his chest. He was vaguely surprised they couldn't actually hear it. He'd never met anyone who could change her appearance so completely. The Elle Gates known to her fans bore no resemblance to the woman he'd been spending his time with. If she slipped away before he got to her, it would be a bitch to track her down, assuming he was able to find her at all. The thought of losing her induced a feeling uncomfortably resembling panic. Losing her would mean…well, it would mean he'd failed a brother *Defensori*, and it would upset Mac's wife. Yeah, that was it.

"Bullshit," Mac rose to his full six and a half feet. Still, Dimitri topped him by inches. "Spill it."

"Look, it's just a hunch, and I could be wrong," Dimitri moved toward the door making a wide path around Kat, hoping it would keep her from picking up on his emotions. He should have known better. Just as he gripped the knob and thought he was in the clear, a small, soft hand landed on his forearm. Kat's nails curled into him like talons, gouging his skin deep enough to draw blood, but the look on her face told him she didn't even realize it.

"I think she's gonna run. I might be off the radar for a while. I'm leaving the bike here for now." Dimitri sent the thought to McAllister telepathically on a wavelength used specifically by the *Defensori,* the warrior branch of the *Earthbound* to which they both belonged.

"Do what you need to do, brother. Get in touch when you can."

Mac stepped up behind his wife, wrapped his arms around her waist, and pulled her back against him. He reached around to pry her tense fingers from Dimitri's arm and then brought them to his lips.

"Back off, Kat. He needs to go, and we're wasting time."

"Whatever is going on, keep her safe, Dimitri," Kat ordered in a firm voice. "I'll have your word on this."

Dimitri regarded the slight, fair woman steadily. He opened his mouth to inform her he didn't take orders from a woman, any woman, but the look in her eyes stopped him. She wasn't trying to throw her weight around; she was simply reacting to her fear. Katrina McAllister was a woman of worth who'd proven herself among the *Defensori* on more than one occasion. Besides, she was Mac's wife and a combination of witch, *Earthbound*, and Archangel in her own right. Realistically, she could probably fry his ass if she ever managed to reliably harness her powers. He nodded shortly, stepped out into the hallway, and disappeared.

****

Kat turned into her husband's embrace and wrapped her arms around his waist. She tilted her head back to meet his gaze, propping her chin on his chest.

"Tell me I'm overreacting, Kassian." Her large, silver eyes pleaded with him for reassurance. "Tell me Elle is going to be okay."

More than anything, Kassian wanted to give his wife the reassurance she craved, but frankly, he didn't know what to think. He'd written Elle off as a necessary nuisance requiring inclusion in his life because of his wife's affection for her. Now not only Kat, but Dimitri too, insisted there was more to the woman than met the eye. He wasn't fool enough to disregard the instincts of two people he trusted with his life.

He dropped a kiss on the top of his wife's silky head and pulled her close enjoying the weight of her body against his. He couldn't tell her what she wanted to hear, but he could tell her one thing he easily accepted as truth.

"Whatever it is, Dimitri will figure it out."

Chapter Three

Elle stuffed the cash filled envelope into her purse hoping it would be enough to hold her over for at least a few weeks. Credit cards and ATM transactions would be too easy to trace if anyone felt so inclined. Eventually, she would transfer all of her funds into an account under another name, but it would have to wait. Taking a deep breath, she reached for the dusty, leather journal and cautiously curled her fingers around the edges, pulling it from the safe. Every time she touched it, she half expected something to happen, a clap of thunder, a bolt of lightning, sudden onset seizures. Something. But in the end, it was simply paper bound in leather. Only the memories contained in the tight, schoolgirl scrawl within its pages were harmful. And only to her. She closed the safe with a decisive click and spun the dial. Setting the book on the floor at her feet, she carefully replaced the panel in the back of her closet, concealing the safe's location, and rearranged all of her flashy designer clothes on the rack in front of it. She wouldn't have any further need for them. In fact, the more nondescript her appearance from now on, the better. She slid the closet door home without sparing a glance at the collection of short, red wigs in various styles stored on the top shelf. She'd already stashed one in her bag in case she needed it in a pinch, but the rest would remain behind. They, too, belonged to a life she could no longer claim.

She retrieved the journal from the floor, checked to confirm the letter remained tucked inside, and deposited it on the bed next to her suitcases. Her instincts told her to keep it close, but she realized it would attract far less attention packed among her clothes in one of the bags she planned to check as soon as she figured out where she was going. Then again, if her luggage got lost, it could be catastrophic. Elle raked her fingers through her loose hair distractedly. Damn, why couldn't one single decision be easy?

Finally, she upended the bag on the bed, scattering the neatly packed contents across the pink, satin comforter in an untidy heap and settled the journal at the bottom of the bag. Nothing about it should provoke comment or invite a strip search, right? She was simply being paranoid. She repacked her hair dryer, a change of undies, her laptop, e-reader, and assorted chargers, and piled them on top of the book. A single black tee remained on the bed, contrasting sharply with the pastel background of the coverlet. She hesitated, feeling a bit silly now to have included it. Dimitri had spilled coffee on it last week, and Elle had offered to launder it. Somehow it had ended up in her drawer, and she'd conveniently forgotten to give it back. She told herself not to pack it, but the thought of waking from the nightmares in a strange place without Dimitri to ground her was daunting. Somehow having the shirt seemed like taking a piece of him with her. She wondered whether he would be disappointed to find her gone. More than likely, he would simply be relieved to have his life back. And Kat? She couldn't bring herself to think about Kat, at all. Their friendship may have started out under false pretenses, but it had become the most important relationship in Elle's life. Taking a deep, shaky breath, she squared her shoulders. She was a strong, independent woman. She'd survived her father's schemes and escaped. She'd eluded her enemies and hidden in plain sight while building a lucrative and successful career. Her luck had held for longer than she ever dreamed possible. She'd survived possession by a demon and an *Earthbound* dagger to her chest. She didn't need a father. She didn't need a guardian angel, a best friend, or anyone. If she repeated the mantra to herself often enough, she might actually come to believe it. Eventually. In the meantime, she would simply do what she had to do and disappear. Hopefully. Her throat ached as she realized it was doubtful anyone would mourn her loss for long. After a heartbeat of indecision, she rolled the T-shirt in a ball and stuffed it down into the side of her bag. If her luggage got lost, she'd need something to sleep in, right?

She dragged her bags out of the bedroom, depositing them outside in the hallway before calling the porter to bring everything down to the lobby. Looking around at the home she'd created, she swallowed hard over the lump that insisted on rising to clog her throat. Her eyes burned as they rested on one item after another, each sparking a memory, until everything finally blurred together. She'd been happy here. She'd built a life. She hadn't asked to be a part of her father's world. She'd simply been unfortunate enough to be born into it. Why couldn't he leave her alone?

She'd been raised believing her father was a

Librarian, part of a secret society who'd been keeping tabs on *Earthbound* for centuries. Their mission was simply to observe and record, but based on what she'd discovered, it was clear at some point their mission had changed. Elle cut her teeth on stories of the *Earthbound* and learned to shield her thoughts from a very young age. As a child, she'd believed it was all a game, the stuff of fairy tales and make believe. Until she learned the truth, a truth she was never meant to discover. When she did, she swallowed her devastation, kept her mouth shut, and bided her time until the opportunity to escape presented itself. She'd smuggled out the journal proactively, hoping never to use it. But now her father had found her again, thanks to the demon, Azakriel. Therefore, Elle Gates had to disappear. It might be her only chance and the letter to her friend would explain everything.

Except once Kat learned the truth, they wouldn't be friends anymore, would they? Still, she'd thought about it long and hard and deep down she knew she owed Kat the truth. And though Elle wouldn't have to witness her reaction, she could easily imagine it, and it broke her heart.

Hopefully, the contents of the journal would soften the condemnation. And if the worst happened, and her father discovered her connection to the others, knowing the truth would neutralize any plans her father might have for using Elle's well-being as a bargaining chip in an attempt to realize his greatest ambition. The capture of a real *Earthbound* to experiment on.

Once she learned how Elle had used her, Kat wouldn't give a flying fig what happened to Elle. And Dimitri…well she wasn't going to think about him either. The biggest favor she could do any of them was to simply walk away.

Her heart heavy, Elle took a final look around and then hitched her purse a little higher on her shoulder. She twisted her long hair into a knot on top of her head and jammed a plaid newsboy cap over it, pulling the brim down low over her forehead. At last, she stepped into the hall, pulling the door closed firmly behind her. The click of the latch echoed in her head with painful finality. No matter what happened, she doubted she would ever return to this place she loved. She hoped she'd been able to buy herself some time with the news conference, well aware that even now, someone could be keeping tabs on her. Her father's message said how glad he was to have found her, how he missed her desperately, and then went on to say she should stay away. A bitter smile twisted her lips. As if she would ever consider returning. Apparently, he was banking on reverse psychology.

As requested, the limo waited at the curb and her luggage had already been loaded. She nodded her thanks to the doorman who stood outside waiting to hand her in and pressed a twenty into his palm before jamming a large pair of mirrored sunglasses on her nose and climbing inside.

She settled back into the comfort of the heavily padded leather upholstery and pressed the intercom to give the address to the driver. If he thought it odd she chartered a limousine and took several heavy pieces of luggage to travel a few miles from her Midtown condo to a small boutique hotel in the Financial District, he kept his opinion to himself, for which Elle was grateful. Ignoring the bustling pedestrians and blaring horns of the bumper to bumper traffic on the streets outside, she pulled her bag into her lap and zipped it open. Insulated from prying eyes by the panel separating her from the driver and the darkly tinted windows, she tugged off the cap and shoved it into her bag, shaking her hair free. Quickly braiding the heavy mass and winding it on top of her head, she pulled out a flesh tone skullcap and blonde pageboy wig. Then she dug into her make-up bag. When she climbed out of the car a few miles later in a narrow alley behind the Federal Reserve, she bore no resemblance to the woman who'd stepped into the car a short time earlier.

The driver came around to open her door. Despite her changed appearance, he barely spared her a glance, and after handing her out, he scurried around to the back to retrieve her bags. She strode into the hotel lobby leaving him to struggle behind with the luggage. Acting oddly nervous, he didn't even wait for a tip before touching the brim of his cap and almost running back to the car as though he couldn't get away from her fast enough.

Elle shrugged at his strange behavior and looked around. It took about five seconds. The lobby was sleek and modern with mirrored walls intended to imply a sense of space, but nothing could disguise the fact that it was barely larger than her closet back at the condo. Between the desk, a potted palm, and the other guests, there was hardly enough room in the cramped space for Elle and her assortment of luggage. She waited patiently while a couple of businessmen in off the rack suits and poorly knotted ties completed their check-in and moved away toward the single elevator at the end of an even narrower hallway, and then she stepped up to the desk.

"I'd like a room for tonight, please," Elle pulled out her wallet.

The young desk clerk, who barely looked old enough to drive, glanced behind her at the pile of luggage and raised a brow. "One night?"

"Yes, please. King bed with a coffee service and fridge if you've got it."

"Sure thing," he tapped the fictitious name and address she provided into the terminal, swiped a keycard, and handed it to her without looking up.

"Credit card, please."

"I'll be paying cash." He glanced up with raised brows, opened his mouth, then closed it again and shrugged.

"That'll be three twenty-nine." He turned to grab the receipt coming off of the printer and handed it to her.

"For one night?" Elle squeaked in surprise. She hadn't actually booked her own hotel room in…well just about forever. Good thing she planned to head out of the city tomorrow. Her available funds would be depleted in no time at these prices. The clerk waited while she counted out the money and then casually informed her she'd have to manage her own bags.

"Sure, no problem," she gritted out between her teeth, shoving the keycard in the back pocket of her jeans and piling her bags one on top of the other. She dragged them the short distance to the elevator and shoved them inside. Poking the button for the eighteenth floor, she leaned back against the carpeted wall with a sigh of relief. She'd made it! Tomorrow she would head for the mountains. Just one more step in saying goodbye to her life, the life she'd created, the woman she'd become. She tried not to think too far beyond that because when she contemplated the prospect of starting over somewhere new, anonymous and alone, it simultaneously broke her heart and scared the living hell out of her.

Fortunately, when the doors slid open on the eighteenth floor, her room wasn't far from the elevator. Elle dragged her bags across the threshold and collapsed on the bed, panting. Two wooden chairs and a small table sat in front of a window that provided a scenic view of a brick wall. Besides a small metal clothes rack and a shelf serving as a nightstand by the bed, a shallow chest of drawers with a coffee maker on top, a mini-fridge, and a wall mounted flat screen comprised the remaining furniture. The décor was a neutral, unassuming beige accented with shades of neutral, unassuming beige. Simple, nondescript, and anonymous. Precisely what she wanted. There was barely enough room to walk, the room's diminutive size giving new meaning to the concept of cozy, but at least it was clean.

Elle hauled herself to her feet, moved to the window to close the drapes, and then clicked on the bedside lamp. A quick peek in the bathroom indicated it was much smaller than hers at home. Her throat tightened again when she remembered she no longer had a home. She swallowed hard and squared her shoulders. She'd find a new home. It was simply a matter of time. She quickly unpacked what she would need for the night, put a couple of bottles of water in the mini-fridge, and carried her toiletries into the bathroom. Now that she'd managed to execute stage one of her semi-formed plan, the strain of the last twenty-four hours announced itself in her stiff and aching muscles. In fact, her limbs felt like she'd been worked over by a two by four and a nagging burn zinged between her shoulder blades, refusing to ease no matter how she stretched and twisted. What the hell, she didn't have anywhere she had to be tonight, right? She cranked on the faucet in the tub until the water was as hot as she thought she could reasonably stand. Maybe a nice long soak was just what she needed. When she finished, assuming she didn't doze off and drown, she'd dig a protein bar out of her bag, toast her new life with a lukewarm bottle of water, and enjoy a long, lonely, and probably sleepless night.

Dimitri waited behind the tinted window on the passenger side of the limo until he saw Elle leave the reception area and head toward the elevator. He'd damn near swallowed his teeth when the unfamiliar blonde hopped out of the car. Damn, the woman could change her appearance at the drop of a hat. He turned to the driver who'd been white knuckling the steering wheel and staring straight ahead ever since Dimitri materialized in the seat beside him around Forty-Second Street. Dimitri suppressed a grin at the cacophony of ideas swirling around in the guy's head. Sure, he could let him go on believing the big scary guy in black was a residual side effect of a bad acid trip he'd taken in the seventies, but it was probably kinder to wipe the guy's memory. Otherwise, the poor bastard might never be the same.

After ensuring the driver would have no recollection of his traveling companion, or the woman he'd chauffeured, Dimitri stalked into the lobby of the small hotel. It required less than a minute of casual small talk with the clerk to read his thoughts and ascertain Elle's room number. Apparently, she'd made quite an impression on the guy, even wearing that ridiculous wig. Horny bastard. Dimitri took a minute to wipe the clerk's mind, as well. What the son-of-a-bitch couldn't remember, he couldn't fantasize about, right?

Dimitri casually strolled in the direction of the elevator. The doors slid open as soon as he pressed the button, but the minute they closed behind him, he decided his way was a lot faster. He faded into the hallway just outside Elle's room. His pulse quickened as he heard her moving around inside. He tamped down his first instinct to simply barge in and demand to know what in the hell she was doing, sensing that approach might be counterproductive. He stepped to the left and laid a large hand on the door of the room next to hers. He closed his eyes and concentrated, confirming it was unoccupied when he sensed no active thought processes from inside. He materialized inside the tiny room and promptly fell over the bed. He climbed to his feet, massaging the shoulder he'd slammed into the chest of drawers and mentally cursed whatever genius had the brilliant idea to take a telephone booth sized room and cram two queen size beds into it. After shrugging off his jacket, he stretched out on the bed nearest the connecting door, shoved a pillow behind his head, and waited to see what Elle would do next.

His mouth went dry as he heard water moving through the pipes in the shared wall. Helplessly, he pictured Elle in nothing but a towel, her long, dark hair tumbling over her soft shoulders. Indulging in the momentary fantasy resulted in his body's instantaneous and painful response. He'd been fighting the connection between them almost from the moment Kassian McAllister dropped her limp, injured body into his arms. He'd waited hundreds of years for a mate, only to discover the first woman who stirred more in him than passing lust was human. Oh yeah, he'd always been a lucky son-of-a-bitch like that! Well, once he figured out what she was up to and knew she was safe, he would walk away. Better to never know that sense of completeness than to spend the next forty or fifty years living under the shadow of impending death. He'd seen the frailty of the human condition up close and personal too many times. There was no way in hell he was going down that road. One brief mortal lifetime just wouldn't cut it. *Nope.* He'd survived this long without a mate, and he could survive centuries more. It just wasn't worth it. It didn't matter that he was *Earthbound* and a licensed physician. There wasn't a damn thing he could do to save this one human woman from her own mortality. The irony left a bitter taste in his mouth. Besides, what woman in her right mind would want a scarred, stubborn, set-in-his-ways project like Dimitri Radchenko? Not a beautiful, intelligent woman like Elle Gates. She could have her pick of men. He groaned aloud and buried his meaty fist in the pillow with enough pent up frustration to send feathers flying everywhere, then sat up with a frown and scrubbed the fluff off of his face. Yeah, that made him feel better. Right.

Hours later, he still alternated between stretching out on the bed and pacing the tight confines of the claustrophobic space while waiting for Elle to fall asleep. He had no idea what she was doing since she held a tight rein on her thoughts even though she was alone. He didn't understand it. Perhaps the years of close proximity to Katrina McAllister with her psychic and empathic gifts made it second nature. It was an unusual talent in a human. A talent Dimitri decided he didn't care for in the least.

Chapter Four

After soaking for nearly an hour Elle climbed out
of the cooling bath, slipped into her nightie, and parked
herself in the uncomfortable wooden chair with a bottle
of water and a couple of protein bars. It wasn't dinner at
the Waldorf, but she had no intention of leaving the
hotel until morning, and the place didn't have room
service. It would have to do. Retrieving a crumpled
paper from the pocket of her jeans, she smoothed it out
on the table in front of her. The message actually
included a return address, as if there was any chance
she could ever forget the location of John Gatewick's
Little Shop of Horrors. Tears blurred the words, and
bile rose to scald her throat. She knew better than to
believe a word of it. *He missed her desperately*…even
as he plotted to capture her. She wasn't his beloved
child. She was an anomaly created in a petri dish. She
shoved the note aside and tore into the wrapper of her
improvised meal.

Chewing until her jaw ached, Elle pointed the
remote in the direction of the television and clicked
listlessly through the channels. Occasionally, she
flicked a glance in the direction of the hulking four-
hundred count, sheeted enemy dominating the room,
mocking her with neat hospital corners. She wanted to
sleep. She needed to sleep. She had little hope she
actually would. The nightmares lay in wait and tonight

she would wake up to a silent, empty darkness. No creaking leather, no Columbian dark roast scenting the air. No Dimitri. She hadn't realized until now how much she depended on the certainty of his presence when she woke, to give her the courage to close her eyes at night.

When both hands on the clock pointed to twelve, and her ass had gone numb from its long sojourn on the unforgiving seat, Elle finally screwed up her nerve and shuffled over to the bed. Turning down the covers, she climbed in with the enthusiasm of a death row inmate being strapped in the electric chair. She fluffed a pillow and slammed her fist into it, creating a pocket for her head. When that failed to produce a comfortable spot, she flipped it, repeated the process, and then tossed the mangled sack of feathers to the floor followed closely by two more. The last pillow proved as uncooperative as the first three. With a groan of frustration, she gathered them all together, tossed them in a heap at the head of the bed and collapsed on top of them.

She tossed, she turned, she moaned, she groaned. At last, she threw her legs over the side of the bed and reached for her overnight bag. Digging out the black T-shirt, she dragged it over her head, tossing aside the satin nightgown she'd been wearing. The damn shirt hung to her knees and was wide enough to go around her twice. Hugging the soft fabric against her skin, she gathered a handful in her fist and held it to her nose. She drew in a deep breath, hoping it still carried a hint of Dimitri's scent. Instead, the April fresh aroma of her laundry detergent made her sneeze. Still, it was better than nothing. Burrowing down into her nest of pillows, she pulled the sheet to her chin, curled into a tight ball, and squeezed her eyes shut.

****

About freakin' time! Dimitri shoved his arms into the sleeves of his jacket and settled it across his shoulders. He'd about given up on the gray, swirling thought patterns indicating Elle had passed into the realm of dreams. His utter boredom made it an effort to keep his own eyes open. Between the hours sitting with Elle, and his nightly hunting expeditions, he'd been getting most of his shut-eye during the day. Today, he hadn't had a chance to put his head down, and fatigue dogged his every movement.

Hoping the set-up in Elle's room mirrored the one he currently occupied, he faded next door while bracing to catch himself should he stumble over anything unexpected. Luckily he calculated correctly, and there was ample space to materialize right inside the door with the bathroom to his right.

Illuminated by the flickering, blue glow of the muted television, Elle slept curled up like a kitten on one side of the enormous bed surrounded by what looked like a pillow fort. Her long, dark hair tumbled around her delicate features like a curtain of silk. She'd kicked off the blankets, and her bare legs tangled in the sheets causing his T-shirt to ride up over one hip, which offered a teasing glimpse of smooth skin and lacy black panties. *His T-shirt?* He refused to speculate on why seeing her wrapped in his shirt caused an increase in his pulse. She'd sneaked away without a word to Kat, or him, or anyone. For all he knew, she could be conspiring against them. He looked at her again, the dark fan of her lashes against her pale skin, her little fist tucked under her cheek, her knees pulled up as though she wanted to make herself as small and inconspicuous as possible, even in sleep. This woman was light years away from the smart and sassy extrovert the public knew. He heaved a heavy sigh. No matter how he tried to spin it, he knew she wasn't the enemy. She was running scared. He couldn't say why he was so certain, but he was. He just needed to figure out who or what she was running from. Then he could fix it and return to his own predictable world where seeing her wrapped up in his shirt as if she was trying to keep a piece of him close didn't twist like a knife in his gut. Hell, maybe he was reading too much into it. She'd probably just been in a hurry and forgotten to pack a nightgown. His gaze zeroed in on a puddle of peach satin next to the bed. Okay, maybe not.

Dimitri sought her mind and found nothing except convoluted, foggy scenes of unfamiliar people and places. He never paid much attention to her dreams, not wishing to invade her privacy. He only intruded when the nightmares began, hoping to somehow erase the memories evoking such fear and pain. But some trauma was too much for even an *Earthbound* to eradicate, and thus far, he hadn't even been able to soften the images that haunted her.

Keeping his mind linked loosely to hers in order to detect the nightmares when they began, he carefully sidestepped along the foot of the bed and squeezed toward the table at the window. He bit back a curse and froze as his leg bumped the bed frame, jarring the mattress. Elle mumbled something unintelligible and rolled over. Hardly daring to breath, he finally made it to the other side of the room without further mishap. Removing his jacket, he folded it over the back of one chair, and then gingerly lowered his body into the other. The small rickety furniture immediately groaned in protest.

Dimitri jumped to his feet and glared at the chair. No way would that pile of matchsticks support someone his size for the next several hours. He glanced at the wrinkled paper on the table, pulling it closer and squinting to read it in the meager light from the television. *Your loving father?* Kat McAllister had said both she and Elle only had each other. Apparently, Elle and her father were estranged. Is that where she was headed? Then why all the subterfuge and sneaking around? It made no sense, but maybe it was something she had difficulty talking about. Lord knows, he had a few of those issues himself. With a shrug, he shoved the note back to the center of the table and straightened.

Propping a shoulder against the wall, he eyed the bed. It was huge—a California King, if he wasn't mistaken—and Elle was a small woman who didn't need much room. He might even be able to snag a pillow without her being any the wiser. The bed would be a helluva lot more comfortable than sitting up in that piece of shit that creaked loud enough to wake the dead every time he twitched.

Awkwardly balancing on first one foot and then the other, Dimitri tugged off his boots. After stuffing his socks inside, he shoved them under the table. He hesitated for a moment and then pulled his T-shirt off too, yanked his belt from the loops of his leathers, and set his keys and wallet on the table. He might as well be comfortable for a change. He left his pants on in the unlikely event Elle woke up and discovered him in her bed. Not that he expected she would. In all the weeks he'd been watching her, she slept like the dead until the nightmares hit.

Taking a deep breath and holding it, he eased down onto the mattress. Lifting first one leg and then the other, he finally stretched out full length, careful to stay right along the edge. The bed was so big Elle looked like she was on the other side of town. She hadn't stirred. She also hadn't surrendered a single pillow. Carefully, he stretched across the vast expanse of mattress and snagged a loose corner of one pillowcase and gently tugged it free. He released the breath he'd been holding, stuffed his prize behind his head, and closed his eyes.

Dimitri's eyes flew open, his lungs struggling for breath, his chest burning. It took him a second to get his bearings and remember where he was. Always before he'd watched the nightmare in Elle's mind in much the same way he would view a movie. This time he must have dozed off with his mind still linked to hers and somehow gotten sucked in.

He was an ancient warrior who'd seen more horrors than most people could imagine, yet the brief immersion into her nightmare had been beyond even his experience. How did she stand it night after night? Elle whimpered in her sleep, and he moved closer. Unable to stop himself, needing to offer her comfort, he reached out a hand to smooth the damp, tangled hair away from her face. His fingers brushed the petal softness of her cheek, and she turned to nuzzle his palm. Dimitri froze, and then slowly pulled back his hand. Elle followed the movement instinctively, rolling in his direction until her body came right up against him. She slung a bare leg over his and draped an arm across his stomach. The moment she touched him, the gray, swirling patterns indicative of restful sleep and normal dreams returned. His heart pounded in his ears, and his mouth went dry. Her nightmares had disappeared at his touch.

Dimitri lay as still as stone, struggling to ignore the warm, moist breath fanning his skin where Elle's cheek rested against his side. His brain had been completely on board with his plan to disregard the bond drawing them together but, if the sudden tightness in his groin and the hot flush creeping over his skin were any indication, his body was ignoring his good intentions completely. He shifted slightly to ease his growing discomfort, and she burrowed even closer into his side. He risked a glance at her face and all of the logical reasons he'd been selling himself for walking away struck him as utterly selfish. For the first time in the many weeks he'd been with her, Elle's expression bore no strain, no tension, and no fear. So many lives he'd been powerless to save, powerless to change. He couldn't change her mortality, but what if he could offer her freedom from her demons? Did he still have the right to walk away just to avoid his own eventual heartache? Scarred, battle hardened, disillusioned, Dimitri Radchenko knew he was no bargain for any woman. He wondered if a woman like Elle Gates would consider him a fair exchange for peace.

"Dimitri?" Her voice was a sleepy whisper.

"It's just a dream, baby. Go back to sleep."

"M'kay," she mumbled and plastered herself even more closely against his side.

Taking a deep breath, Dimitri carefully lowered his arm and rested his hand on her nearly naked hip.

Gritting his teeth against the silky texture of her skin, he pulled her into him. She sighed softly, and his heart twisted, battling a war between contentment and consternation. Elle Gates was human, fragile, doomed, her limited lifetime a blip on the radar of his long existence. Nothing but pain awaited him. And hell, considering she was human, there were no guarantees the bond had any effect on her at all. This attraction could be all one sided. Still, in this time, at this moment, he couldn't deny it. Holding her in his arms and thinking of her as his felt…right.

Mac's wife had put her faith in Dimitri to keep her friend safe, and he fully intended to do so. Even if he couldn't quite decide whether his determination to protect her stemmed from his promise to Kat or his own desire. It was irrelevant at the moment. Something had this woman spooked enough to run from a successful career, everything and everyone she knew and loved, without a word. As the first faint fingers of dawn stole through the gap in the drapes and inched across the room toward the bed, Dimitri reluctantly disentangled himself from Elle's arms and gathered up his things. With a lingering look at her peaceful face, he faded from the room with plenty of questions but absolutely no answers.

****

Elle extended her arms over her head and indulged in a long, satisfying stretch as she came awake, keeping her eyes tightly closed against the intrusive morning light. *Morning?* Shooting straight up in the bed, she looked around, blinking back tears of disbelief. Her nose wrinkled at the faint scent of leather knowing her mind must be playing tricks. She hugged the black tee, henceforth known as her lucky shirt, against her. A full night of demon free sleep! She hardly dared to believe the nightmare could be over. Well, one nightmare perhaps. Reality slammed her in the side of the head as she blew out a long breath and slung her legs over the side of the bed. There was still the small matter of her *father* to contend with.

Still, sometimes a girl just had to take what she could get, and for now, a good night's sleep and twenty-four hours free of demonic memories felt pretty good. Elle bounced from the bed and bent to retrieve her nightgown from the floor where she'd dropped it the night before. But it wasn't there. She straightened from her crouch and gasped as her now alert brain registered the appearance of the room. Her nest of pillows was on the *other* side of the rumpled expanse of linen, exactly where she'd stacked it. One pillow, however, had apparently migrated clear across the bed and bore the imprint of a head. Leaning closer, she reached to pluck a stray hair standing out in sharp contrast to the pristine whiteness of the pillowcase. The hair was longer than hers, and it was darker, straighter. Elle sat down hard as the room spun and her stomach flipped. It hadn't been a dream. Dimitri Radchenko had spent the night with her in this bed. Her heart fluttered into her throat, stealing her breath. How had he found her? Why?

She took several deep breaths until her heart resumed a normal rhythm. Maybe she was wrong. Maybe it *was* her hair and she was just letting imagination run away with her. *Or indulging in wishful thinking.* But if she was right, if Dimitri had been here and could find her so easily, despite all of her precautions, so could anyone else. She needed to move quickly, and in order to do so, she needed to travel a lot lighter. After folding the black tee carefully and replacing it on top of the journal in her bag, she pulled on the jeans she'd worn yesterday and topped them with a lightweight ivory sweater. She hurried to the bathroom, washed her face and brushed her teeth, gathered her hair into a ponytail, and carried all of her toiletries back in the room and tossed them into her bag. Sinking her teeth in her lower lip, she braced herself against the weight and heaved her three remaining suitcases onto the bed, dumped them out, and began the painful process of downsizing. She crammed her few remaining possessions into her overnight bag, and removed the luggage tags with her identification from the others, dropping them to the bottom of her purse. Things were only things, after all. Unlike people, things could be replaced. Assuming she lived long enough to need them.

Chapter Five

Elle clutched her purse and overnight bag to her chest as she navigated the narrow aisle of the bus, and sank down in the very back seat with a groan of relief. She slid over to the window and dumped her bags on the seat beside her to discourage anyone from getting the idea she welcomed company. Port Authority had been crowded, as usual, but she didn't notice anyone paying particular attention to her as she navigated the ticket counter and hurried along the red and white tiled corridors to her gate. Her gaze continued to bounce anxiously around the terminal. Attuned to every movement, she examined every face, until she had finally been able to board. At this point, she suspected everyone and told herself she was relieved she hadn't had a single glimpse of six and a half feet of leather-clad angel, either.

The midday sun beating through the glass warmed her skin uncomfortably, and the skullcap beneath the wig already felt damp and tight. From past experience, she knew she would be the proud owner of a full-blown headache long before she reached her destination. Resting her head against the back of the seat, Elle tugged a bottle of water from the pocket on the side of her bag and took a long pull. In less than two hours, she would be at Katrina McAllister's family home in the Pocono Mountains. She planned to deposit the journal among the boxes of old books from Kat's cousin's estate. Once she mailed the letter, Kat would know where to find it. Elle counted on the fact the books were all still stacked and forgotten in the basement. She would be far more careful this time. She wouldn't open a single book, wouldn't look at a single page, and she *absolutely* wouldn't read anything out loud. Demonic possession was an experience probably best confined to once in a lifetime.

Elle pressed her nose against the side window for a last glimpse of the skyline as the bus emerged from the Lincoln Tunnel and barreled into the traffic heading west on Route 3. Her breath fogged the glass, obscuring the sight of everything and everyone she was leaving behind on the meager finger of earth known as Manhattan. The thought of a forever goodbye squeezed her heart so painfully she thought it might be preferable if it stopped beating altogether. Elle looked away from the window and slumped down in her seat. Maybe, by some small miracle, her sacrifice of giving up everything she walked away from, would buy her some redemption with the people she loved. Assuming they were ever able to get beyond her act of betrayal.

Craning her neck, she looked out the back window at the bumper to bumper traffic that resembled a parking lot as they merged onto Route 46. It was impossible to tell if someone tailed the bus in the massive congestion, and she didn't see a single man with long, dark hair streaming behind a set of wide shoulders while perched on a roaring, chrome death machine. She hadn't really been expecting to see him, but the fact she specifically looked forced her to admit she'd been half hoping. She pulled a set of earbuds from her purse and plugged them into her phone. Once the bus reached the I-80 junction and headed into Pennsylvania, the traffic would drastically reduce and she'd be able to spot a tail better. She brought up her playlist, poked the buds into her ears, and stared sightlessly out the window at the miles of car dealerships and strip malls whizzing by.

Elle awoke with a start to the sound of her own cry, a lump in her throat and her stomach churning. People in the seats closest to her turned in her direction to regard her with openly curious expressions. Apparently sorrow, stress, and the rocking motion of the bus had lulled her to sleep. And right into the nightmare. Naturally. A bead of sweat tickled the valley between her breasts as hot blood rushed into her face. She offered the observers a weak smile as reassurance. She hated that she had so little control over her own mind. Maybe she should start wearing Dimitri's shirt full time? Whispering among themselves, the passengers turned back to face the front of the bus. Except for one.

Elle bit back a curse as a disheveled, sandy haired man who appeared to be a few years older than she, rose to his feet three rows in front of her. He stumbled in her direction, grasping the tops of the seats to maintain his balance against the uneven sway of the speeding bus. He towered over her, clutching the seat with one hand and awkwardly pushing his thick, black framed glasses up on his nose with the other. His wrinkled khakis, an oversized polo shirt, and cross-body man purse completed his ensemble. Elle wondered why he didn't just get the word Geek tattooed on his forehead.

"Are you okay?"

"Fine, thanks." She looked away, staring out the window and hoping he would take the hint. He didn't. He shifted from one foot to the other until she looked back. He glanced pointedly at her bags occupying the seat next to her as if hoping she would make room for him to sit down. As if.

"I, uh…well, I wondered if you ate today? I get hypoglycemic myself, and you look a little shaky." He offered a shy smile and dug around in his bag. He held out a cellophane package. "I always carry snacks. Would you like some crackers?"

"No, thanks. Really, I'm fine," Elle replied firmly. She crossed her arms over her chest and hugged herself, trying to shake off the feeling of unease. Constant paranoia was exhausting. The guy seemed harmless enough. Maybe it was just the aftereffects of the dream.

"Well, okay…" He dropped the crackers back in his bag and shoved his glasses up on his nose. "If you're sure."

"Really, no thanks." Elle poked the earbuds back in her ears. Retrieving her sunglasses from her lap, she shoved them back on her face in a clear sign of dismissal. Still, the man continued to stand there, clutching the seat and swaying over her dangerously. She was about to lose her thin veneer of politeness and tell him to get lost when he frowned and turned to stumble back to his own seat, throwing a glance over his shoulder every so often until he finally sat down out of sight.

Elle tugged the earbuds free and shoved them back into her purse along with her phone. Then she turned to look out the back window. Now that they had crossed into Pennsylvania, the traffic had thinned considerably.

In fact, it was downright sparse. The long, straight stretch of road flanked by thick stands of trees visible through the back window of the bus sported a couple of SUV's, a minivan crammed with family vacation equipment, and a white cube van about a half a mile back. The inevitable eighteen-wheelers were the only other vehicles on the road. She turned back to face the front and glanced at her watch. Her head throbbed persistently now, and she could hardly wait to ditch the wig and free her heavy hair from its confinement.

With nerves strung taut as a tightrope, Elle heaved a sigh of relief and gathered her things together preparing to disembark as the bus finally slowed and pulled into the terminal. She was one short cab ride away from Kat's place and hopefully the next stop on her road to obscurity.

****

Dimitri cruised past the entrance of the low brick building serving as the Mount Pocono bus terminal and pulled the battered cube van into the parking lot a little further along. Squinting through a pair of mirrored aviators, he observed every passenger alighting from the bus and committed them to memory. Once Elle entered the building, he tossed the sunglasses on the seat beside him and removed the baseball cap he'd donned over his newly trimmed hair. He raked his fingers through the sweat dampened strands now hanging just below his shoulders. Hell, his hair hadn't been this short since World War II. His size and his scars made it hard enough to blend into the general population. A thick mane of black hair hanging nearly to his ass pretty much negated his ability to go unnoticed. He couldn't do much about the first two problems, but the hair had been an easy fix.

He climbed down from the cab as Elle came out of the building and dropped a bag at her feet near the curb, keeping her purse securely hitched on her shoulder. He wasn't especially concerned she would recognize him from this distance should she happen to look in his direction. Hell, at the moment, he barely recognized himself, and his hair had little to do with it.

Dimitri had never felt so torn between opposing loyalties. For hundreds of years, he'd pursued a single-minded course of action with a defined purpose. Protect his brethren, avenge his family, and thwart the *Fallen*. Now, one small, kick ass sexy woman threatened to undermine his resolve. If he discovered Elle Gates was somehow working against the *Earthbound*, would he have the strength to hand her over to face judgment and simply walk away? The decision was no longer as clear as it should be. Aside from her obvious physical appeal, he'd seen her courage, grit, and determination as she fought to come to terms with an experience that, according to the *Fallen* who'd given his life to destroy the demon, no human should have been able to survive. Kat told them her empath had felt Elle fighting to keep the demon in check, to counter the evil, even as he ravaged her mind and body. A guy couldn't help but fall for a woman like that. Dimitri's gut twisted. Despite his best intentions, human or not, this woman had come to mean something to him. Period.

A taxi pulled up to the curb where Elle waited, and as she climbed in, Dimitri reached inside the truck for the sunglasses, jamming them back on his face. Then he tucked the keys over the visor as arranged, and slammed the door. Her cab pulled away and took off down the road. He wasn't concerned about losing sight of her. He could travel a hell of a lot faster his way. He'd figured out her intended destination almost as soon as the bus crossed the Delaware Water Gap. What he couldn't figure out was why. He propped a shoulder against the dented fender of the borrowed truck, squinting into the late afternoon sun despite the UV protection until the car rounded a turn and disappeared from sight. Then he slapped the Yankees cap back on his head, tugged the brim down over his eyes, and faded to Kat McAllister's house. He hoped when all was said and done, Elle Gates was playing ball for the home team.

Chapter Six

The crowded trees blurred together along the side of the road as dappled sunlight randomly pierced the thick, green canopy, flashing like a strobe light and irritating Elle's already throbbing head. She had neither the energy nor the interest to acknowledge the cab driver's droning attempts at small talk, though she supposed he was trying to be friendly or angling for a bigger tip. She shifted uncomfortably to alleviate the prickly irritation of the stiff, cracked, vinyl seat poking through her jeans. Instead, she concentrated on taking shallow breaths, hoping to minimize the pungent mixture of stale smoke and unwashed bodies permeating the close confines of the vehicle and burning her nose. A loud cough interrupted her stupor and she turned to see the driver regarding her curiously over his shoulder.

"We're here," he repeated a little more loudly.

Elle's cheeks warmed as she realized they'd pulled into the gravel drive of the rambling two-story farmhouse and she hadn't even realized they'd stopped. The white clapboard building huddled among the trees looking as if it had occupied the spot forever. She loved it here, nearly as much as Kat did. The wooden swing twitched eerily on one side of the enormous wraparound porch as though someone had jumped out of it to run inside and announce her arrival. Must be her overactive imagination, of course. Just one of the many perks of living in the hallucinatory world of sleep deprivation and paranoia.

"Fourteen fifty," the driver said as he climbed out and lumbered around to the rear of the car. Elle climbed out on the other side, digging in her bag for her wallet. Hinges creaked, and the car rocked as the trunk slammed shut and the driver came around to where she waited.

She took the lead and the cabbie followed, shuffling up the drive with her bag. A mild breeze carried the faint scent of lilacs. According to her father, they'd been her mother's favorite, and the fragrance brought thoughts of a mother to mind. A mother who had technically never even existed. She had no idea why she thought of that now. She didn't want to think about her make-believe mother, or Kat, or…anyone else for that matter. In fact, she was tired of thinking. If she could manage to think of nothing at all for a couple of hours, that would be great.

Reaching the bottom of the porch steps, Elle turned and tugged her bag from the driver's meaty fist and set it on the sidewalk beside her, then handed the man a crumpled twenty. He glanced at the bill and reached in his pocket for change.

"Keep it," she snapped in a curt tone. The guy narrowed his eyes as if trying to get a better look at her. Elle ducked her head, letting the smooth curtain of the wig fall forward and partially obscure her features.

"Thanks for the help. Have a good night."

He hesitated, looking as though he might have something more to say, but finally nodded and made his way back down the walk and along the drive. At least the guy could take a hint, she thought. She hadn't intended to be rude. She was tired, that's all. Bone weary, soul sucking tired in a way she doubted any amount of rest could remedy.

She waited until the cab pulled away, then bent to pry a loose board from the steps and retrieve the key Kat always left there. Dropping her bag in the entry hall, she closed and locked the door behind her then leaned against it with a relieved sigh. The hallway led straight back to a spacious but outdated kitchen. To the left of the hallway was a cozy living room and behind it, a formal dining room with a large, heavy table which had been Kat's grandmother's and dated to the late twenties. Every piece of furniture was old, mismatched, and well used, but the overall feeling was warm and welcoming. A collection of framed photographs lined the mantel of the stone fireplace exactly where they'd been for as long as Elle could remember. Elle sagged against the door and let the peace she always felt in this house envelope her, relieved to see that despite her marriage to a wealthy man, Kat had left the place completely unchanged. Just one more thing that would make it hard to say good-bye.

Elle let her purse slide from her shoulder to join her carry-on on the floor and headed for the half bath off of the kitchen. She availed herself of the facilities and after washing her hands and splashing some water on her face, she regarded herself critically in the mirror. Her lashes couldn't conceal the faint blue smudges beneath the wide, blue eyes staring back at her. The harsh glare of the fluorescent lighting gave her already fair complexion a sickly pale translucency. Elle sighed. Even after the first good night's sleep she'd had in recent memory, the bags under her eyes had bags of their own. She tugged off the wig and skullcap and freed her sweat dampened hair, combing it with her fingers, and let it fall in a tangled riot of waves around her shoulders.

Shuffling back into the kitchen, she decided it was too bad she hadn't had the presence of mind to have the cab driver stop at a grocery store for a few staples. It looked like her overdue dinner would consist of the one remaining protein bar left in her purse and a nice, refreshing glass of tap water. Expecting nothing, she peered into the fridge. A half-empty bottle of flat root beer, a gallon of spring water, and a full can of coffee nearly made her shout for joy. Not surprisingly, there was no milk, but at least she had the promise of caffeine. She also found a jar of mayonnaise, a bottle of ketchup, and two kinds of mustard which hadn't yet passed their expiration date.

A quick survey of the cabinets produced a can of tuna, some saltine crackers, and an unopened jar of dried, minced onions. Hallelujah! Elle made quick work of putting together a makeshift meal with the tuna, spices, and mayonnaise and wolfed it all down with half a sleeve of crackers and a glass of syrupy root beer.

After returning the kitchen to its former order, Elle trundled back out into the hall and eyed her bag critically. Head down to the basement and deposit the journal now? Or enjoy this gift of temporary peace and deal with the problem in the morning? Decisions, decisions. Peace being a rare commodity lately, Elle decided to embrace it and dragged her bag over to the sofa. She pulled out the book stuffed with the envelope and laid it on the coffee table. Then she pushed it away from her slightly as though it might jump up and bite her. The journal and the letter held every truth she'd never wanted anyone to discover, and now she planned to confess all. It would have been easier to simply disappear without a word, but it wouldn't have been fair. She owed Kat the truth. Better late than never.

The unexpected knock caused her stomach to leap into her throat. Startled, she jumped from the sofa, banging her knee painfully on the table. Heart racing, she limped quietly toward the door, trying to remember if she'd locked it. Then she realized how ridiculous she was being. If someone waited outside to threaten or harm her, they'd hardly bother to knock, right? Taking a deep breath, she clicked the deadbolt to the left but left the chain intact, just in case, and cracked open the door.

"You! What are you doing here?"

Nerd-nuts from the bus pushed his glasses up on his nose with his forefinger and looked down at his shoes as the color crept up his neck and into his face. Elle saw him reach for his man purse and started to close the door. He stuck a foot in the crack to stop her.

"Wait, please! I'm sorry. I know I probably seem like some crazy stalker, but I'm a big fan, Miss Gates and I wondered if you could sign a couple of books for me?" He pulled out one of her contemporary romances and a hardcover of her investigative account of Jack the Ripper and held them tentatively in her direction.

"You have *got* to be freakin' kidding me!"

"My name is Jim, by the way. I thought it was you on the bus, but I wasn't really positive until this. He tucked the books under his arm and pulled his phone out of his bag. After tapping the screen a few times, he turned it in her direction. A photo of herself stared back at her, one he'd obviously taken as she exited the bus, except the hair was red. "It looked like you, but the hair threw me off. Once I played with color in the photo editor, I knew I was right."

"No offense, Jim-by-the-way, but yeah, it does occur to me you're some kind of crazy stalker, and I'm sorry, but you've got the wrong girl."

"But…" Elle pushed his foot out of the way with hers and started to close the door. The man pushed back. For a geek, he was a lot stronger than he looked. A knot of fear tightened her stomach. "Please, if you could just sign…"

"Honey," Elle called back over her shoulder, annoyed at the tremor she heard in her voice and hoping her *fan* didn't notice. She'd never had any sort of problem, but she knew other authors who had. One woman in particular was actually forced to take out a restraining order against an overzealous reader who'd been unable to separate the writer from her sexy female characters. "Could you please come out here and throw this lunatic off the porch? He thinks I'm some writer or something."

Jim's eyes widened behind his Buddy Holly specs as he attempted to peer behind her. "Look. I don't want any trouble." He slowly backed away from the door.

"Then I suggest you leave before my boyfriend comes out. He's taking a nap, and he's *really* grumpy when he wakes up. It's the steroids, you know. I told him he should give them up, but he's really into that whole more is better muscle mass thing."

Jim-by-the-way shoved his books and his phone into his bag, tripped down the steps, and ran for his bike without another word. Elle closed and locked the door, then leaned against it and released a breath, waiting for her pulse to slow and her knees to stop knocking together.

Her attention was diverted by a movement of the drapes on one side the front window. Elle straightened slowly and picked up her journal, as it was the nearest weapon at hand. She moved quietly toward the window. The house had been closed up for months and heaven knew what wild creature may have found its way inside from the surrounding woods. Taking a deep breath, she tore the curtain aside and discovered a squirrel crouching behind the fabric. Startled, he stared up at her with his beady little eyes, then scrambled from behind the fabric and started running a manic marathon around the room.

"Oh, my God!" Elle screeched, swatting the air with the book in the animal's general direction. "I am *not* a nature girl you little tree rat! Get out! Out!"

The rodent continued to run frantically around the living room, up and over furniture, under tables, everywhere, in fact, except anywhere near the door. Elle dove for her purse and fumbled among the contents until she came up with a small canister of pepper spray. Hoping it wouldn't seriously hurt the animal, but praying it would at least stun it enough to allow her to throw a towel or something over it and shove it out the door, she waited until it paused for breath on the back of the sofa. The creature eyed her warily, whiskers twitching, and tail erect. She could see its tiny little heart racing against its tiny little chest, the wild rhythm matching her own. She felt a momentary twinge of guilt, then she decided she had enough of her own fear to deal with at the moment and the erratic heartbeat probably indicated the damn thing was rabid or something. She crept forward, aimed carefully, and depressed the button. She missed the animal completely, the stream striking the wall as the frightened creature launched itself from the sofa, limbs extended as though flying. It landed directly on Elle's chest.

****

Dimitri's eyes had never left Elle's slight form as she climbed from the cab and walked stiffly to the front of the house. Well concealed in the small thicket of trees standing between the house and its nearest neighbor, he frowned as she bent to retrieve a key. He expected Mac would have put a stop to his wife's sad lack of security by now. On the other hand, the McAllisters hadn't spent any time here in months, as far as Dimitri knew, and aside from items with sentimental value, he doubted there was much of anything worth stealing. Hell, even now, Mac said his wife insisted on doing her own grocery shopping and continued to use coupons despite their wealth. His frown dissipated, replaced by a smug grin as he realized she probably did it more to annoy Mac than for any other reason. He liked Kat McAllister more all the time.

Dimitri scrubbed a hand over his face, wondering when he'd suddenly become so easily distracted by the contemplation of relationships, and returned his attention to Elle. Creeping forward, his gaze scanned the area closer to the house for a place to hide. Then he straightened to his full height with a growl. Why skulk around out here like some crazy stalker, anyway? It would be a hell of a lot easier to protect her if he knew what exactly he was protecting her from. It was high time Elle Gates understood she could run, but she couldn't hide. At least not from Dimitri Radchenko. He would simply walk right up to the front door and demand answers.

He faded to the front porch, stepped up to the door, raised his hand to knock, and then hesitated. Okay, so maybe he'd give her a couple of minutes to get settled in before totally pissing her off. Not that he was especially *concerned* about pissing her off. He was just trying to be considerate. Yeah, that was it. He decided to kill a little time by working his way around the house, being careful to duck under any windows. The place was a security nightmare. There were at least a dozen ways to get into the place, and that was assuming you were human and didn't have the added advantage of being able to fade. He circled the place again, this time working his hands in intricate patterns around the house as he set protective *sigils* in place, which would keep out anyone except those whose molecular signatures he'd woven into the ancient angelic characters.

As he started back around the opposite side of the house, to weave the *sigils* around the front, a flash of movement near the road caught his eye. A bicyclist turned in the drive and dismounted. As the man removed his helmet, Dimitri immediately recognized the wrinkled khakis, oversized polo shirt, and thick, black framed glasses. The guy had gotten off of Elle's bus at the terminal.

Dimitri crept to the side of the porch, flattened himself against the house, and watched as the visitor climbed the steps and approached the front door. A bubble of rage simmered in his chest as he considered for the first time perhaps Elle wasn't running *from* someone, but *to* someone. But this guy? Seriously?

Listening to their exchange, it was all he could do to stay hidden and refrain from jumping up on the porch and choking the stupid out of the creep. Then he found himself biting back a smile. She was quick on her feet. He'd give her that. He swallowed a laugh as the guy tripped down the stairs and ran for his bike.

As soon as he was out of sight, Dimitri faded into the trees along the road. Two hundred yards away a black van idled along the shoulder and as bike boy approached, Dimitri saw the side door slide open. The guy was yanked off the bike and dragged into the van leaving the bike to tumble into the ditch at the side of the road. Dimitri faded closer for a better look. Then he felt the unmistakable shocks traveling up and down his spine signifying the presence of evil. There were either *Fallen* or some of their *animorti* puppets in that vehicle. What were they doing here? Dimitri palmed his stilettos from the intricate tattoos on his forearms and prepared to move in.

And then he heard the scream.

Chapter Seven

Expecting anything, Dimitri faded directly into the house still clutching his weapons. The first thing he noticed was the front door standing wide open. The second was a shrieking Elle dancing madly around the center of the living room with a shell-shocked squirrel clinging desperately to the front of her sweater.

The hilarity of the sight made him temporarily forget about the van and its occupants. Making no attempt to hide his amusement, Dimitri allowed a low rumble of laughter to build in his chest as he slapped the knives against his forearms where they faded back into the ink. Tattoos really were a handy way to carry a weapon. He let out a piercing whistle between his teeth capturing the attention of both Elle and the squirrel. The animal looked relieved. The woman, not so much. The squirrel scampered up Elle's chest and over her shoulder to hop into Dimitri's outstretched hand where it happily crouched, quivering with an expectant expression of near adoration.

Dimitri stepped to the open door, squatted, and released the animal onto the porch. Straightening, he closed it and turned back to the woman standing wide-eyed and speechless in the center the room. She smoothed her palms along the front of her sweater and tugged down the hem with visibly trembling hands before clearing her throat and taking a step in his direction.

"What are you doing here?" she whispered.

"Saving your ass apparently." He grinned. "Seriously, woman, you survive a demon and lose it over a squirrel?"

"Well, rodents carry diseases, you know," she huffed, twisting a lock of her dark hair around and around her finger. "And did you see those teeth? They were...well, they were really big. And sharp. And big. Anyway, how did you do that?"

"Do what?"

"Get the damn thing off of me? He hopped right into your hand like you were his new best friend."

"Yeah, well, I have a way with animals." Dimitri felt the heat rush to his face. In fact, if there was an injured animal within a five mile radius, it honed in on Dimitri Radchenko like a drunk to whiskey. It didn't do a helluva lot for his badass reputation to be interrupted in the middle of a raging battle by an injured animal seeking comfort. But shit like that happened. All. The. Time. And his brother *Defensori* took great delight in busting his chops about it. Frankly, he couldn't understand why anyone considered it a big deal. He always took out more than his fair share of the evil ones before turning his attention to the animal.

"Obviously. Who knew? I should have been calling you Dimitri Doolittle all this time." Elle quipped with a faint smile.

Dimitri shrugged. "Grew up on a farm."

"Really? You never told me that."

His jaw clenched. There were a lot of things he'd never told her. Didn't seem to be much point in dredging up ancient history. He'd find the *Fallen* responsible for the death of his parents and everyone else he'd known...eventually. He didn't know the name the bastard went by these days, but the face was burned into his brain. If the son of a bitch still lived, he would know him on sight. It was simply a matter of time, and he had plenty of it. Elle's eyes searched his face and then dropped to the book and envelope at his feet. He saw a flicker of something—fear?—before her expression hardened. "Well, kudos on your timely appearance, Doc, and thanks. But now you need to go."

"Is that right?" He replied in a deceptively mild voice, crossing his arms over his chest and glancing down at the clutter. Then he looked back at Elle who stood with her arms hanging limply at her sides, though her fists clenched and unclenched spasmodically. "Well, how about I help you clean up this mess, and then we'll talk about it?"

"No!" She cried hurrying forward and gathering up her things as he stooped to do the same. "I mean, I'll get those. Really, Dimitri...go kill some bad guys or something. I just need a little time alone, okay?"

Dimitri examined her pale face. Clutching the book against her, her chest rose and fell rapidly, and beads of sweat dotted her forehead. Most telling was the fact she couldn't meet his eyes. He reached to wrap a hand around the side of her neck, burying his fingers in her hair and tilting her face up to meet his gaze. His breath caught at the desperation he saw there.

"I promised Kat I'd keep you safe, and I keep my promises, so I guess you're stuck with me. Now maybe you'd like to tell me why you're being watched by *animorti*."

"What?" Her face went a shade paler.

"You heard me. I killed two of the lousy bastards in the garage under your building this morning. Naturally, I thought they'd followed *me*. But, your little friend who stopped by for a visit just now was picked up down the road by a couple more. So spill it, Elle. Why are there *animorti* keeping tabs on you?"

"I, uh, I've no idea," she whispered faintly, dropping her eyes.

"You're a very bad liar, Elle."

She swallowed audibly, then took a deep breath and wrenched herself away from him. Stepping back out of his reach, she laughed bitterly as her features contorted. Shuffling through the book she gripped tightly in her hands, she tugged an envelope free.

"Actually, I'm an excellent liar. My entire existence has been nothing but one big, fat lie after another. I'm trying to do the right thing for everyone, but clearly you aren't willing to walk away and let it go. So, here." She shoved the envelope into his hand then walked over and tossed the journal on the sofa before spinning back to face him. He glanced down at the envelope.

"What's this?"

"That's it, that's everything. The whole ugly truth sealed up in a neat little package. Knock yourself out. I'm going to take a shower, so I'll just say goodbye now as I don't expect you'll be hanging around after reading it. If you could pass it along to Kat, I'd appreciate it. Tell her…" her voice cracked and she swiped at her eyes. Dimitri curled his fingers into a fist to keep from reaching out to her. "Never mind. I guess there really isn't anything to say."

She stepped around him and started up the stairs.

"It can't be as bad as you think." He moved to follow her, but she held up a hand to stop him and her throat convulsed.

"Yeah, it can," she croaked. "Goodbye, Dimitri…and thank you. I didn't deserve any of it, but I do appreciate everything you've done for me. I-I think I'll really miss your big leather-clad ass."

Before he could say another word, she turned and stumbled up the stairs as though all the hounds of Hell were on her heels. He tapped the envelope nervously against his thigh. After stepping out to the front porch and finishing up his *sigils* to secure the house, he came back inside, strode to the sofa, and dropped onto it. Hard. The pipes gurgled in the wall as the hot water from the boiler in the basement was called upon by the shower upstairs, and still he continued to turn the sealed missive over and over in his hands. Well, he'd wanted to know what was going on, right? But now after seeing her reaction, he wasn't so sure. He blew out a deep breath in a long, low whistle and slipped a finger under the seal, carefully sliding it along the seam. Elle seemed convinced the information in this envelope was catastrophic. It couldn't possibly be as bad as she thought, could it?

Five minutes later, with his pulse pounding in his ears and his jaw clenched tightly enough to crack teeth, he reconsidered his initial assessment. He needed air. Leaving the pages to flutter to the floor unheeded, he stormed from the house, slamming the door nearly off of its hinges behind him.

****

Elle flinched as the force of the slamming door shook the house. She'd been expecting it, but that didn't make it hurt any less. Dimitri was gone, and the life she'd known was truly over. Her plan hadn't gone exactly as she intended, but the end result was the same. The truth was out, and there was no going back. Surprised to discover she actually had any tears left, she turned her face into the spray and let the anguish consume her as she waited for the water to wash her sorrow and regret down the drain.

Both the sun and the hot water were long gone by the time Elle hauled herself from the shower and pulled on an old robe of Kat's she'd found hanging behind the door. Dragging a brush through her wet hair, she peered into the steam fogged mirror. Yep, her eyes could easily pass for the bloodshot golf balls they felt like. It wasn't an attractive look, but then again, there was no one here to impress. Elle originally planned on spending a few days at the farmhouse until she could figure out her next move, but since Dimitri already had plenty of time to get back to the city and fill Kat in on the truth, it now seemed more presumptuous than ever to stay. Besides, according to Dimitri, she was being watched. She gathered her things, took them into Kat's old room, and dumped them back into her bag. It was too late to go anywhere tonight. She'd enjoy one last night in this house that had once been a home and leave first thing in the morning. Destination unknown.

She shrugged off the robe and hung it on the back of the closet door. Then she pulled Dimitri's shirt over her head, poked her legs through a pair of silk boxers, grabbed her bag, and headed downstairs. Dropping her bag in the hall, she flicked on the lamp and saw the pages of her letter to Kat littering the floor where they'd fallen. Apparently, Dimitri had decided to simply give

Kat the gory details in person without any of the emotional bullshit that probably came through in the letter. Didn't really matter. There wasn't any way to make it pretty. She gathered the loose pages together, shoved them back into the envelope, and tossed it on the coffee table. She would give Kat the option to read it herself, along with the journal, if she ever chose to do so. With nothing left to do, she curled up on the sofa and pulled an afghan over her bare legs.

She simply lay there, staring at the ceiling. She knew she should be making plans for her future, but she couldn't stop thinking about her past, the people she loved, the people she'd hurt, the people who were now lost to her forever. She threw a forearm across her aching eyes to block out the light from the hallway. Her head throbbed, too. In fact, everything seemed to hurt at the moment. But nothing hurt half as much as her heart.

****

Dimitri propped his boots on the front porch railing. After reading the letter, he'd slammed out of the house and stomped the perimeter of the yard like a raging bull, seething with an almost pathological need to tear her father limb from limb. What kind of father uses his daughter as a lab rat? The son-of-a-bitch was damn lucky Dimitri didn't know where to find him. Yet.

When he'd calmed down enough to think straight, he'd sent his mind out in search of hers and discovered Elle was still in the shower. As she appeared in no hurry to emerge, and trusting his *sigils* to protect her for the short time he planned to be gone, he faded to a small convenience store a couple of blocks away and picked up a few things. He also surveyed a one mile perimeter around the property and didn't see any sign of the van or feel even a whisper of evil. Whatever their reason for being in the area, the *Fallen* had cleared out for the time being. When he returned to the house, he decided it might be better if he cooled his heels for a while until could speak without verbally crucifying her bastard of a parent.

He didn't need telepathy to know she was crying. He could hear her through the old parlor windows, which were badly in need of re-glazing. He splayed a hand across his chest and rubbed at the uncomfortable twinge her grief caused. If her ailment was physical, he could fix it. Emotional torment? Yeah, not really his specialty.

He should probably at least let her know he was still here, since she probably assumed he'd taken off. Hauling himself to his feet with a grunt, he grabbed the grocery bags and rolled his head on his shoulders to loosen his tense neck muscles. Approaching the front door with all the enthusiasm of a condemned man walking to the gas chamber, he crossed the wide expanse of the porch. His slow, measured footsteps echoed on the wooden planks. Reaching the door, he shoved both bags into one arm and curled his fingers around the knob. He drew in a deep breath and blew it out slowly. He had no clear idea of what he would say, no idea what she needed to hear. He would just have to wing it. Yeah, this should go well. He turned the knob and stepped across the threshold into the dimly lit hall.

Dimitri's head exploded. At least it felt that way as the pepper spray caught him just under the chin, soaking the front of his shirt and sending fumes and fallout everywhere. His skin burned like he'd been face planted on a hot grill. Thank God, she hadn't hit him directly in the eyes. Still, the substance was a potent irritant, and his body reacted immediately. It was impossible to avoid inhaling it unless he stopped breathing altogether. His eyes clamped shut automatically, leaving him temporarily blinded, and tears poured from beneath his tightly closed lids. His nose streamed, his chest heaved, and a fit of coughing damn near sent him to his knees as the irritated cells in his throat and lungs tried to rid themselves of the chemical. It had been years since he'd taken a shot of pepper spray. He hadn't liked it much then, and he liked it even less now.

His first instinct was to rub the offending substance away, but he knew that would only spread the burn and make it worse. Keeping his hands away from his face through sheer determination, he dropped to his knees and began to rummage blindly in a grocery bag. Somehow he forced his eyelids open wide enough to find the milk and pop the lid. He tipped his head back and poured the milk directly onto his face, feeling the almost instantaneous relief as it neutralized the burn.

He blinked rapidly and turned to face his attacker. Elle's shapely bare legs poked out below the hem of his shirt, and he could detect just a hint of pebbled nipple through the thin cotton. Her thick, dark hair was a riot of tangles, and her bare feet were braced shoulder width apart as she gripped the small canister at her side. Her lips formed a perfect "O" and her blue eyes were wide and swollen, surrounded by tear spiked lashes. His groin twitched in involuntary response. It was official. He'd lost his mind. He had to be nearing the point of insanity if he stood here just shy of respiratory arrest getting aroused by the woman who'd caused it.

"What are you doing here?" she gasped.

"Wondering the same thing myself at the moment. Do you think maybe you could put that shit down before you accidentally hit me with it again?" He wheezed. "Fortunately, I heal fast so I'll be fine in a couple of minutes, but I'd rather not repeat the experience."

"What? Oh…" Elle flushed, then turned and set the canister on the hall table. "Well you said I was being watched, and I thought… I didn't expect you to come back."

"Yeah…well, surprise. Grab the bag, will you?"

Dimitri climbed to his feet slowly, grabbing one bag and nodding at the other. He strode into the kitchen without waiting to see if she followed, deposited the bag on the kitchen table, and began rummaging through the cabinets. After locating the dish detergent, he squeezed a generous amount into the sink and began filling it with cool water. Then he tossed in a kitchen towel. He heard Elle shuffle into the kitchen behind him, and the crinkle of the grocery bag as she set it on the table. He plunged his entire head into the sink a couple of times, twisted the excess from his hair, and then squeezed out the water and detergent from the towel and draped the cool cloth over his face and neck with a barely suppressed groan of relief.

"Dimitri, I… I'm really sorry." He felt the heat of her body mere inches away. "Does it hurt much?"

"Had worse."

"Isn't there anything I can do for you?"

Dimitri peeked over the towel. Eyes wide and her usually smooth forehead puckered in a worried frown,

Elle stood close enough to kiss. He could think of more than a few things he'd like her to do for him but figured now was probably not the best time to mention them. The way she nibbled on her lower lip made him wonder what it would be like to hold it between his and do exactly the same thing. Between the fullness in his groin and the pepper spray all over his chest, his upper and lower body were in an all-out war to see which of them could cause him the most misery.

"Um, why don't you come and sit down over here while I go wipe up the mess." The chair legs grated against the tile floor as she stepped away and pulled it out for him. "There's milk all over the floor."

Dimitri held the towel over his face with one hand and groped his way across the kitchen until he felt the back of the chair, then fell into it heavily. Actually, *Earthbounds'* accelerated healing being what it was, he felt better already, but if she wanted to take care of him a little, he could live with that. Besides, worrying about him seemed to have taken her mind off of everything else for the moment, so he continued to play along.

"Yeah, sorry about that. The milk neutralizes the stuff. I wouldn't mind a glass for my throat if there's any left." His voice still sounded raspy, but at least he could breathe again.

"Oh, uh, sure." He lowered the edge of the towel and watched as she crossed to the cabinet. His shirt rode up as she reached for a glass, providing him with a tantalizing glimpse of her firm, rounded bottom in the silky boxers. She filled the glass with milk and set it carefully in front of him, reaching for his hand to guide him. She jumped when he pulled back sharply.

"No, don't. No sense both of us being in misery."

He reached for the glass and raised it to his lips as he let the towel fall onto his chest.

Elle left him sitting in the chair and snagged another towel from the drawer. She stepped into the hall and stooped to mop up the puddle of milk, keeping her back to him.

"I'll get that." He pushed back the chair and followed her to the hall.

"Done," she announced briskly. Wadding up the saturated towel and gripping a rung of the stair railing, she pulled herself back to an upright position. Turning back toward the kitchen, she found him standing so close behind her she nearly bumped her nose on his chest. She quickly took a step back and tugged at the neck of her shirt.

"Listen, you think you could help me get my shirt off? It's saturated with the stuff."

"You expect me to believe you can't take your own shirt off?" Elle eyed him doubtfully. "I hope that's not one of your standard pick-up lines. Have to tell you, Big Guy, I've heard better."

Chapter Eight

Dimitri's laughter was warm and intimate, and far too appealing for Elle's fragile peace of mind. She took another step back just to be safe when she felt a warm tendril of desire curl low in her stomach. It was official. The strain had finally pushed her over the edge. She was losing her mind. She was the last person Dimitri Radchenko would ever want. Especially now. In fact, not only was she shocked to see him back, he didn't even appear upset with her. It made absolutely no sense.

"I can't take it off over my head. It'll just re-deposit the pepper oil on my face. It needs to be cut off, straight up the back. You'll have to be careful not to touch it. You have gloves or something?"

"Oh." She ducked her head and stepped around him to get gloves and scissors from the kitchen, relieved he was behind her and couldn't see her burning cheeks. She simply couldn't believe he'd actually come back. Maybe he hadn't finished the letter? Or maybe he failed to grasp the implication? She found the scissors in the cutlery drawer and a pair of rubber gloves under the sink. She pulled the heavy yellow gloves up over her forearms. They were far too large for her hands, and she had difficulty getting her fingers into the handles of the scissors. Finally, she managed to get a good grip and turned to Dimitri, who'd again come up behind her.

"Just cut it straight up the back?" She asked hesitantly.

"Yep, right up the middle," he confirmed turning his back to her and sweeping his hair forward over one shoulder and out of her way.

Elle bit her lip in concentration, pulled down on the hem of the T-shirt, and began sawing away at the material while fighting to ignore the smooth, tanned, and oh so touchable skin being revealed inch by glorious inch. The gloves made it awkward, but little by little, she started to make progress. Dimitri stood patiently with his thumbs hooked casually in the front pockets of his leathers as the material gave way.

"There!" Elle announced triumphantly as the scissors cut through the neckband and the two sides of the shirt fell away from one another. She tugged off the gloves and returned them to the basket under the sink.

Dimitri carefully pulled the shirt forward and away from his irritated skin without comment, folding the dry sections around the part still wet with pepper spray. He grabbed an empty grocery bag from the table, shoved the ruined garment inside, tied the bag closed, and deposited the whole thing in the trash bin near the back door.

"Thanks."

"No problem"

That wasn't strictly true. Elle decided it might be a tiny problem. Her gaze locked on the mesmerizing expanse of exposed chest as Dimitri turned back to toss the wet towel in the sink. She'd seen the stilettos tattooed on his forearms many times. All *Defensori* carried their chosen weapons in a similar fashion. The lines inked along the left side of his ribcage were a new discovery, however. The script was intricate and elegant, beautifully done, and she wondered what it said. She quickly averted her eyes when he caught her staring and busied herself with putting away the groceries he'd brought. She half squashed the loaf of bread, gripping it tightly to disguise her shaking hands. It must be the aftereffects of thinking her father's people had found her. It had absolutely nothing to do with the tempting package of rippling muscles now exposed to her view. Nope, nothing at all.

"I don't know what I'll do with all this food since I'm planning on leaving tomorrow."

"Hungry?" Dimitri asked as though she hadn't spoken. Okay, she could play ignore the big purple elephant in the room, too.

"What? Oh, I uh, had some tuna earlier."

"Well, I didn't and I'm starving. Check the last bag. I picked up a couple of Italian subs."

Elle dug out the sandwiches and set them out on the table while Dimitri retrieved two cans of cola from the fridge where she'd put them. He popped the tab and plunked one down in front of her before pulling up a chair for himself. He tore into the wrapper and wolfed down half of his sandwich before Elle had even managed to get the paper off of hers. Then he tipped the aluminum can to his lips and chugged down at least half of it before pausing for breath. Elle quickly returned her attention to her sandwich when she realized she'd been staring in fascination at the way his throat worked as he swallowed the drink. The tangy scent of vinaigrette combined with the pungent kick of salami tickled her nose, and her stomach rumbled in response. She carefully picked the thin strands of sliced onions off the top and placed them in a neat pile on the edge of the wrapper before taking a hefty bite. She barely suppressed a moan. The fresh roll, perfect ratio of meat to cheese, juicy tomato, and crispy lettuce all combined into a mouthful of deliciousness that beat the tuna hands down and tasted like the best thing she'd eaten in days.

Elle munched contentedly as Dimitri shoved the last bite into his mouth, crumpled the wrapper into a ball, and scored two points in the trash before leaning back in his chair.

"You cut your hair."

"Never let it be said you don't have amazing powers of observation."

"Well, I was a little preoccupied." Elle protested around a mouthful of her second dinner. "It looks good. Of course, I liked it before, too."

"You did?"

"Suits you, I guess." Elle shrugged and took another bite. How many times had she fantasized about the way all that hair would feel tangled around her bare skin? She grabbed the can and took a long drink as she started to choke. She glanced across the table and prayed she'd remembered to keep her shields in place when the wayward thought had crossed her mind. Dimitri took a long drink of his own soda and simply continued to watch her eat. She felt like a mouse being observed by a wily cat. A cat biding his time.

Neither of them spoke again until Elle finished her meal and got up from the table to throw her wrapper and their soda cans in the trash. She'd just turned back to her chair when Dimitri broke the silence.

"About that letter…" he began. And there it was.

Elle felt the floor tilt. She swallowed forcibly as the sandwich threatened to come back up and say hello and took a deep breath to steady herself, but discovered it had little effect. She dropped unsteadily to the chair.

"You didn't read it did you?" She rasped. "I should have known when you came back."

"I read it."

"Then I don't understand," Elle cleared her throat and laced her fingers together in her lap. Her throat tightened to the point her voice was a strangled whisper when she spoke again. "If you read it, you know what I am, what I've done. Why would you come back?"

Dimitri folded his arms across his chest, his broad, bare chest, and his brows slammed together. "You can't really believe you're the one at fault in this whole scenario?"

"Why wouldn't I?" She jumped to her feet and began pacing in a circle, needing an outlet for the nervous energy. "I'm a liar and a fraud. Kat struggled so badly with her abilities, with being different. I knew what she was, or at least suspected, and I never told her. She trusted me and I used her to hide from him. Some friend, huh?"

"And what if you'd told her the truth back then about who and what she was? Do you really think she would have believed something so far-fetched?"

"I should have given her the option."

"Elle, you're not the bad guy here. You're the victim. What your father…"

"Don't!" Her throat tightened further, to the point of pain, and she took deep, gasping breaths that did nothing to quiet the roiling nausea suddenly erupting in her gut. She began to shake. A random, full body trembling that buckled her knees and threatened to send her to the ground. "I'm not a victim, and he's not a father. I'm a science fair experiment, genetically engineered, cultured in a petri dish, and gestated in a stranger's uterus. I'm not even a person. I'm a madman's creation."

There, she'd said it out loud. Her private fear, the one she'd kept hidden all these years. She was little more than a modern and more attractive version of Frankenstein's monster. She hugged her arms across her chest as though she could hold herself together and wobbled on rubber legs to the sink where she stared sightlessly through the kitchen window into the darkness. She couldn't look at Dimitri. She doubted any piece of her heart remained unbroken at this point. Still, seeing the look of disgust he must surely be wearing would decimate any small piece that might be left intact.

"You have *got* to be kidding me," he drawled. "Children are born by in vitro fertilization all the time. So, you're telling me they're not people?"

"Of course, they are! That's entirely different." She had never really considered the comparison before. But it couldn't be the same thing at all, could it?

"How so?"

"Well, they weren't created out of greed and a desire for power."

"That may have been *his* motivation, but it wasn't yours, and the technical details of your conception don't mean shit. The why isn't important, the how isn't important. What's important is that it doesn't define you, and it isn't who you are. You didn't let it. You took Gatewick's ideologies and threw them back in his face."

"Well, I'm pretty sure it was Azakriel who threw them back in his face," Elle's lips twitched in a wry smile. "All these years I've been working to prove to myself I was more than just his creation. I guess I needed validation that I was worth something no matter how I came to be. Deep down, I must have wanted him to know I'd succeeded on some level, or the demon wouldn't have found the suppressed desire in me and contacted him to let him know. Anyway, I assume that's how he found me."

She heard the chair legs scrape against the floor and then Dimitri's warm breath ruffled her hair. It would be so easy to give in to temptation and simply lean back into him. Just for a minute. She craved someone to hold her, someone to help carry this burden. She gripped the edge of the counter and fought the urge. Now that he knew the truth about what she was and how she'd lied, surely he would leave. The little piece of her heart that began to want something more, the tiny spark of hope she'd been clinging to, sputtered and died the moment he'd slammed out of the house. *But he'd come back, hadn't he?*

His hands came up to rest on her shoulders. Squeezing lightly, he turned her around to face him. Trapped between the counter and his body, she kept her eyes down, refusing to meet his gaze. She realized her mistake when she saw his leathers had slipped low around his hips, and she couldn't help but be fascinated by the tempting cut of corded muscle tracing along his hips and disappearing into his waistband. Her hands were pinned between them, and her fingers tingled as they brushed the smooth skin of his flat stomach. It felt just as silky and warm as it looked.

Judging by his swiftly indrawn breath, he felt the same awareness. She quickly pulled her hands away and fisted them at her sides.

"Well, Elle, you've more than proven you're worth something, though I doubt anyone except you ever questioned it, so why would you even consider returning to that bastard?"

"What?"

"I saw your father's note. Last night at the hotel. You left it lying on the table. Is that where you were headed?"

"You *were* there! I knew it!"

"Just answer the question," he countered without admitting to anything. "What would ever possess you to go back?"

"I never intended to go back. I briefly considered it because I worried they would find out about Kat and try to get to her if I didn't. But then I realized he has no idea who he's dealing with. Kat hasn't even scratched the surface of her powers yet, and McAllister would never let any of them get close enough to touch her. But, I had to make sure someone knew what he might be up to before I disappeared. I planned on leaving the information here for Kat to find. If Gatewick is any example, I don't believe the *Librarians* are a bunch of doddering old historians scribbling on parchment anymore, Dimitri. They're technologically advanced. They want what you have, what you are. They want to build a better man."

Dimitri exhaled a long, low whistle. "So they've progressed from recording history to trying to dictate it? Transhumanists?"

"Maybe. I've run across that term during my research, and the ideology seems similar. As far as I know, up until the time I escaped, Gatewick only managed to successfully produce one genetically engineered offspring. Uh, yeah, that would be me. But, the DNA doesn't appear to have transferred *Earthbound* abilities or longevity as he'd hoped. I believe that's the ultimate goal."

"Why didn't you just tell Kat what was going on? Or me? Why run?"

"It's one thing to anticipate her reaction. It's something else entirely to stand there and watch it evolve on her face when she realizes how I used her."

"Used her? I think you underestimate her. Kat McAllister loves you like a sister. I've seen it."

"She loves who she thinks I am. I was raised in an environment that was pretty isolated from the 'real world.' Gatewick always told me his work was dangerous, that there were those who would kill for it, those who would use me against him. I had no reason to doubt him. I was a kid, what did I know? It was the only life I'd ever known. I was seventeen when I learned the truth. I'd been in his office reading. Books were the only friends I had back then."

"And…?" Dimitri prompted softly when she hesitated.

"I was supposed to have been in bed hours before, so when I heard Gatewick coming, I panicked and hid. I overheard him dictating his research notes and put two and two together."

Elle shrugged, offering no hint of the utter devastation which accompanied the discovery that her whole life, her very existence, was simply a fabrication to advance the power of a group of fanatics. Many times in her life Elle had felt alone, but never as completely as in that single overwhelming moment of clarity, when she understood she was nothing but a commodity to the only father she'd ever known. Whatever awaited her in the outside world, it couldn't compare to the threat of her everyday existence.

Chapter Nine

Elle swallowed hard, finding it difficult to speak over the tightness in her throat. She'd never shared the intimate details of her upbringing with anyone, and she wasn't sure why she did so now. Maybe because she'd kept it sealed inside for so long that, like an overheated pressure cooker, it had to blow. At this point, she had nothing left to lose. She risked a peek at Dimitri, afraid of what she would see on his face. He stared down at her intently. Unbelievably, his forehead appeared creased in concern, not revulsion.

"And that's when you made the decision to escape?" Dimitri prompted.

"Yeah. God, I was *so* stupid, *so* naïve."

"You didn't know anything else. Can't beat yourself up for that."

"Still." She shook her head and took a tired breath. "Once I knew the truth, I became desperate for a way out. I'd been homeschooled...the big old threat of the outside world, you know? Finally, when I turned eighteen, I convinced Gatewick to let me attend a small nearby college to take some classes. I told him I thought maybe I wanted to be a writer. I guess he didn't find it all that surprising given my love for books. I think maybe he even saw it as something I could pursue in relative isolation, something that would keep me content, while still keeping me under his thumb. For a full year, I went to class every morning and came home every afternoon as though everything was perfectly normal. And he watched me like a hawk. I didn't give him any reason to doubt me. All the while, I kept busy figuring out how to create a new identity and disappear. And then I met Kat. She'd recently lost her mom and seemed as much a loner as I was, but we clicked. Kindred spirits, two lost souls? I don't know. I guess she was drawn to me partly because I wasn't freaked out by her abilities. Of course, I had the advantage of knowing about *Earthbound,* and once I realized what she could do, I began to suspect what she might be. I cultivated the friendship, and when the time came to make my move, I showed up at her door and claimed I was on the run from an abusive father. She took me in and hid me, no questions asked."

"Well, it wasn't exactly a lie, baby."

"No, but it wasn't exactly the truth either, was it? And I never told her my suspicions about her origins even though I watched her struggle every day. What kind of friend does that? I was selfish, Dimitri. I should have told her the truth about herself *and* about me, but I was afraid she'd reject me, and I had nowhere else to go. I counted on the fact Gatewick would expect me to run as far and as fast as I could. I guess I was right. If it wasn't for the damn demon, I might have avoided him indefinitely, I think."

"What possessed you to go messing with those books of Miranda's in the first place?"

"Kat's cousin was a witch. I figured they were spell books of some sort. I hoped to find a way to kill Gatewick from a distance. I never dreamed I'd unleash a damn demon."

"What exactly did you think you'd accomplish even if you found something? You aren't a witch."

"Well, duh! Too bad you weren't there to point that out sooner since we see how well my plan worked out."

She flinched slightly as he reached out to stroke her cheek with his thumb. "You aren't a killer, Elle. You wouldn't have been able to go through with it even if you'd found a way and the demon hadn't interrupted your plans."

"Well, I guess we'll never know, will we?"

Elle kept her gaze pinned on her feet, and he stepped even closer until the length of his body pressed flush with hers, pinning her against the counter. She did look at him then. His obvious arousal was unmistakable and incomprehensible. She glanced pointedly in the direction of his crotch and then back to his face.

"You can't be serious! After everything I've just told you…were you even paying attention? How could you possibly want…me? You don't even know who or what I am. Hell, *I* don't even know who or what I am."

"*I* know exactly who and what you are. Oh, and don't plan on disappearing again anytime soon, either. You aren't going anywhere without me."

"You do seem to have an uncanny knack for showing up exactly when I need you," Elle whispered. "I know you promised Kat you'd protect me, but now that you know the truth, I think it lets you off the hook. There's no reason to take what I'm sure you consider your duty so seriously."

"Yeah, I did promise Kat, but it's not why I'm here."

Elle tilted her head back and looked him square in the eye. As her gaze connected with his, a shock of awareness ran through her, something raw and primal. In that moment, the rest of the world fell away and there was only Dimitri. She wanted this man, and not just because he was trip-over-your-own-feet sexy. There was so much more to him, even if he wasn't willing to admit it. Even if she was the only one able to see it.

"Why *are* you here, Dimitri?"

He cupped her face in his big hands and buried his fingers in her hair. The question filled his eyes, and she didn't hesitate to raise her face to his. This might be her only chance, all she would ever have of him.

His breath feathered along her jaw before he covered her slightly parted lips with his own warm, firm ones. His mouth settled on hers, and she melted against him allowing the kiss to deepen. She'd spent so much of her life keeping people at a distance, but Dimitri made her want to let someone in. She hesitated. Her fingers curled tightly against his stomach, but then she gave herself up to the riot of feelings the kiss evoked and allowed her hands to slide up the hard planes of his chest, twine around his neck, and tangle in his hair. His arms came around her waist, and he pulled her more intimately against him. The hard evidence of his desire pressed insistently against her stomach, and she was lost. Need flickered along the surface of her skin, seeped into her bones, and exploded somewhere deep in her soul.

Mine. The thought flashed unbidden from his mind into hers.

As she pressed her soft curves against him with a sexy little whimper, Dimitri's world condensed and spun away until he knew nothing except her soft, plump lips under his, the faint lemony scent of her hair, and the soft brush of her fingertips on his neck. He pointedly ignored the panicked little voice in his head reminding him she was human. Human or not, every good intention of keeping his distance evaporated the minute his lips touched hers. Damn, but she tasted even better than he'd dreamed. His tongue traced the seam of her lips and she opened willingly, letting out a sexy little moan in the back of her throat as his tongue swept inside and he deepened the kiss. His mouth slanted over hers again and again like a dying man discovering a bubbling spring in the desert. After seven hundred years, this sure as hell wasn't his first trip to the rodeo. But he quickly discovered it might as well have been. She wasn't just any woman and this wasn't just any kiss. This was a *holy shit, I am so freakin' screwed* kiss.

He harbored no illusions about what the future would hold if he continued down this road. The ghosts of all those he'd failed in the past rose up to mock him. He'd lived long enough to lose nearly everyone who'd ever mattered to him. Despite his gifts, he'd been helpless to save most of them. And when old age or disease arrived to claim her, he would be helpless to save the woman in his arms. Shit, *Earthbound* or not, one wrong move and a Hell blade could end his life just as easily, right? He might be able to give himself every good reason in the world to walk away from her, but the bottom line was he didn't want to. She filled a place in him he hadn't even realized was empty. Nothing was guaranteed, nothing but this, nothing but now. If the best he could hope for was a few decades, maybe he should get over himself and grab it. Could he really stop dwelling in the past, anticipating the future, and concentrate instead on the sweetness of the present? He wasn't sure he had it in him anymore, but this woman sure as hell made him want to try.

When he lifted his head at last, they were both breathing raggedly. Beneath her half closed lids, Elle's blue eyes darkened to the deep indigo of a stormy sea, and her lips were red and swollen from his kisses. She dropped her forehead against his chest as though she needed the support to stay upright. Her hands splayed across his stomach, the heat of her like a brand on his skin.

"You didn't answer my question," she whispered.

Apparently, she didn't realize he just had done exactly that, and maybe for now, it was better she didn't. From the moment she'd been dropped into his unsuspecting arms, he'd been walking around in turmoil, the attraction to her a constant ache in his gut. They were as different as night and day, but then neither one of those things could exist without the other, right? He rested his chin on top of her head, took a deep breath, and simply breathed her in. *Mine.*

"You know, baby, I kinda counted on you to have a little common sense."

She tipped her head back and smiled ruefully. "Common sense is not as common as you might think, *baby*. And in my case, all I can say is, wow, you really shouldn't have put your eggs in that basket, huh?"

He pressed his lips to her hair, then leaned back and tipped her chin up with a finger.

"So why didn't you tell Kat the truth after you'd established your own life and didn't have to worry about being thrown out?"

"I wanted to. So many times. But by then I just

didn't know how to begin. She'd become my family, my person, all I had, and I was afraid of losing her."

"Yet you were planning to run away."

Elle shrugged. "In the end I realized I would rather lose her than put her, or any of you, at risk. I don't know where Gatewick got the DNA samples for his research, but I believe with every fiber of my being he'd give his eyeteeth to get his hands on an actual *Earthbound* for his experiments. He has to be truly mad, Dimitri. I realize that now."

"How are the *Fallen* involved?"

"I don't know. Until you told me about the *animorti*, I didn't realize they were."

"I'm gonna call Mac and fill him in." Her smile faded and shadows replaced the light in her eyes.

"Why?"

"Seriously? You didn't think we could let that asshole continue with business as usual, did you?"

"I guess I didn't really think about it. What are you planning?"

"Not exactly sure. Clearly Gatewick still wants you back, and it's up to me to make sure he doesn't get you." He gave her a rib-cracking squeeze.

"I think I should be insulted, you large, ill-mannered angel," Elle gasped, pushing against his chest. "It's not up to you, at all. I've been taking care of myself for a very long time, and you aren't responsible for me. The last thing I want to do at this point is put anyone I care about on Gatewick's radar. And please remember while I supposedly have the correct DNA, I don't have any *Earthbound* characteristics. When you crush me, I will *not* heal up good as new in five minutes or less."

"Duly noted." He relaxed his grip slightly but didn't release her from his embrace. "That journal you're so attached to, it wouldn't happen to contain Gatewick's research notes, would it? We have our own experts, you know. His notes could provide some valuable information."

"The book is nothing more than an old diary of mine. I thought maybe if Kat read it…I don't know, maybe she would understand what my life had been and find a way to forgive me eventually. I didn't steal his research. I didn't have to. I *am* the research."

"Self-preservation is a helluva strong motivator, and I'm telling you, Kat won't condemn you for it. But, I meant his records…you know, the actual data."

"No, but I know where he keeps it."

"Well, you sure aren't going back in there to get it." Dimitri frowned while lightly running his thumb along the soft skin of her inner wrist near the base of her thumb. "What the hell…?"

"What?" Elle jumped nervously.

"Feel that?" Dimitri gripped her fingers in his and ran them over the area until she detected the small bump resembling a grain of rice.

"I never noticed it before. What is it?"

"My guess is a microchip of some kind. Maybe you took more information than you thought when you escaped. Maybe it's all stored right in here." He tapped her wrist. "And if that's the case, he's got to be desperate to get you back." Dimitri pulled her back into his arms as a chill settled over him. If the information on that chip was valuable, Gatewick had nothing to lose. He wouldn't even need Elle alive as long as he could get his hands on her body. Well, hell would freeze over before that happened. She might not understand it yet—he wasn't even sure he understood it himself—but the only one getting his hands on Elle Gates' body from now on was one Dimitri Radchenko, *Earthbound* angel and *Defensori*.

"Okay," Dimitri took her by the shoulders and turned her toward the hall. "Go up and get dressed. Then throw that shirt back down for me since you trashed mine. I'm gonna call Mac and get us a ride out of here. Then we'll figure out what to do."

"Maybe you could go talk to McAllister, and I could just stay here tonight? I know you must think I'm a complete and total coward, but I'm finally waking up to the fact my whole plan was pretty hare-brained, and I should have just come clean to begin with. And now that I actually have… Look, I know I have to face the consequences, but I'm just not ready right this minute. Dimitri, I—"

"Go get dressed and let me worry about the consequences. Go!" He gave her a gentle shove and swatted her behind. Inordinately proud of the fact he resisted the urge to grab a handful of the firm, rounded flesh he could feel through the thin fabric of the boxers, he waited until she'd gone through the hall, grabbed her bag, and hurried up the stairs, throwing worried glances at him over her shoulder every few steps. He'd like nothing better than to spend the night here with her. On the other hand, there were *Fallen* involved and they knew, or at least suspected, she was here. He had complete faith his *sigils* would hold, but he wasn't willing to risk her life on it if the evil ones decided to attack en masse. He yanked out his phone and punched in Mac's number.

Pinching the bridge of his nose between his thumb and forefinger, he propped a hip against the counter and waited for Mac to pick up. He'd reassured Elle over and over that Katrina McAllister would understand. He honestly believed it, but truth be known, he didn't know the woman well enough to make any guarantees. His gut tightened as the call clicked through. He sure as hell hoped his instincts were right.

"McAllister."

"Hey, Mac. I think maybe we've got trouble. But first you better put your wife on the phone…"

Chapter Ten

Elle didn't care for flying. She discovered she enjoyed it even less strapped into the seat of a glass bubble bobbing in the night sky and zipping toward the city lights at a mind-numbing rate of speed. She'd been expecting a limo. McAllister, in his typical over the top fashion, sent a chopper. Elle anticipated she would have an hour or two to gather her wits before facing the McAllisters. Apparently, she would only get about twenty minutes.

Spine ramrod straight, icy fingers twisted together in her lap, she felt Dimitri's eyes on her, but kept her face turned away. Tears pricked the back of her lids as she admitted to herself for the first time that she actually cared for the big lug. She'd hoped maybe he'd started to care for her just a little bit, too. But that was before. Now he knew Elle Gates was a nothing more than a character in a book, an actress in a play, an illusion in a magician's nightclub act. She'd donned the persona all those years ago and clung to it like a sniper to an assault rifle. Oh sure, he'd kissed her, but it was probably nothing more than a little misplaced lust, right? Still, he'd called Kat and explained the whole mess to try and make it easier for her. She understood a part of him was a leather wearing, deadly weapon packing, night stalker prowling the alleys and seedy bars killing *Fallen* and their *animorti* servants. But that was a Dimitri she didn't know and could barely fathom. That wasn't *her* Dimitri. She drew in a long, shaky breath. Was she nuts? He wasn't *her* Dimitri.

"Radchenko."

Elle glanced over, surprised to see the phone plastered to his ear. She hadn't even heard it ring over the sound of the wind.

"No shit?" He continued. "Well, that's a lucky break. Okay, see ya in a few."

Dimitri clicked the phone off, shoved it back inside his jacket, and then turned slightly in the limited confines of the cabin to face her.

"Green isn't really your color, you know," he shouted over the roar of the chopper.

"Excuse me?"

"You look like you're about to hurl." He smiled and reached over to untangle her fingers, enveloping her frigid hands in his large, warm ones. "Take a deep breath, woman. Blood and guts may not faze me, but I don't do vomit. You're making yourself sick for nothing. It's gonna be okay, you'll see."

"It's not that. Well, okay, it *is* that, but not entirely. Actually, I'm not a very good flyer."

Dimitri's dark brows slammed together. "Well, hell! Why didn't you say something? Mac planned to send a car. I asked for the chopper so we could get back into town faster. I figured the sooner we got this confrontation over with, the sooner you'd realize you were worried for nothing, and the sooner you'd be able to relax."

"Oh."

"We'll be back on the ground soon." He squeezed her hand. She appreciated the reassurance, but of course once the flight ended, she had the whole confrontation thing to deal with. No matter what he said, she couldn't really believe it would be anything less than awful. She'd replayed several versions of the coming scene over and over in her mind since Dimitri had placed the call. In some, Kat was the pale and silent picture of devastation and Kassian McAllister ranted and raved, flushed and fuming on his wife's behalf. In others, it was Kat who flew at her in a fury while McAllister simply stood back and let her have at it. Elle knew he'd always merely tolerated her for his wife's sake. None of the versions concocted by her imagination ended well. While she didn't agree with his take on the situation, maybe Dimitri had inadvertently done her a favor. Perhaps, like tearing a bandage off of a festering wound, quick and painful was the way to go. Drawing it out didn't really hurt any less.

"That was Mac, again." He continued. "His brother Alec is flying in tonight. Alec isn't a *Defensori*, but he's got some connections with the *Librarians.* He's also trying to get hold of Galen. You'd never know it by looking at him, but he's a technology geek. He should be able to tell us exactly what's on that microchip."

"Alec's not a *Defensori*? But Kat told me he helped McAllister and Luca rescue her and Callista from Jacques Rapier."

"You don't grow up a McAllister without learning how to fight," Dimitri chuckled. "But, technically Alec isn't a soldier. He's the family academic."

The chopper banked sharply to the left and Elle's stomach pitched and rose into her throat. She swallowed a mouthful of sour bile that burned all the way down and instinctively tightened her fingers in Dimitri's when the lights of the helipad on top of the McAllister building appeared below and they began their descent.

Lower and lower, they dropped out of the night sky like a stone. Elle vaguely perceived Dimitri's voice, but she didn't register the words. Her heart thudded so wildly, she barely felt the jolt as the skids made contact with the roof and the craft bounced to a stop. Her attention remained riveted on the woman on the rooftop standing stiffly in her husband's arms watching their arrival. The wind generated by the whirling blades of the aircraft tossed her silvery hair around her face, obscuring her expression.

"Drop your shields," Dimitri advised as he unbuckled his safety harness and brushed Elle's fumbling fingers away to free her from her restraint. "Kat's empath will feel the truth, but Mac might take a little more convincing. Let him see what he needs to know."

"Swell," Elle whispered through lips gone dry as Dimitri hopped to the ground and reached back for her. His large hands spanned either side of her waist as he swung her out of the copter, keeping his head down as the blades continued to whirl. She clutched his jacket, waiting for her shaking legs to support her, and he kept one hand at her waist while he reached back with the other to grab her bag. As soon as they were both clear, he signaled the pilot, who took the chopper back into the air and headed off in the direction of the airport.

"Okay?" Dimitri asked quietly. Elle glanced up and searched his face. She detected no condemnation in his expression, no anger, only the same unexpected concern she'd seen earlier. She didn't believe she deserved it, but she was incredibly grateful for it at the moment. She swallowed past the lump in her throat and nodded. Taking a deep breath, she dropped every shield she'd ever built. The air began to swirl around her again but the chopper was long gone. The hair on the back of her neck crackled with electricity and gooseflesh rose on her arms. Hearing a strangled gasp behind her, she squared her shoulders and turned out of Dimitri's arms to face the storm.

Kassian McAllister had taken a step back from his wife, presumably to avoid being burned by the white-blue sparks spewing from her fingertips like Fourth of July sparklers on crack. Kat's hair rose in the air and floated around her face like a wild tangle of spun silver and her eyes were alight with an otherworldly glow as fascinating as it was frightening.

"Shit," Dimitri hissed close to her ear. "Behold the Archangel in a snit."

"Put your damn shields up," McAllister roared. "She's absorbing your memories and she can't control the anger."

"Ooops, my bad." Dimitri's tone wasn't the least contrite. In fact, he sounded oddly amused. Elle slammed a mental wall into place and would have turned to ask exactly what he could possibly find humorous about the situation, but she couldn't tear her attention away from her friend. Kat's hair slowly settled around her shoulders and the finger fireworks sputtered and died.

"Arabella Penelope Gatewick, I am *so* going to kick your ass," Kat called as she shook out her hands with a grimace while stalking across the roof in their direction. McAllister followed right on her heels, his expression darker than any thundercloud.

"Penelope?" Dimitri burst out laughing.

"Not. Now." Elle hissed, frantically searching Kat's expression as she drew closer for any hint of softening or forgiveness. Instead of icy rage, Kat's face was damp with tears and splotchy from crying, and Elle's heart contracted sharply knowing she was to blame for the pain so plainly visible on her friend's face. She raised her chin slightly, fully prepared to accept whatever venom Kat launched in her direction. Still, as Kat's arms came up, Elle instinctively took a step back into the solid wall of *Earthbound* behind her and Dimitri's arms closed around her protectively.

Kat halted and cocked her head to one side.

"Dimitri, please unhand that stupid, stupid girl. I'd like to kill her now," Kat demanded mildly. After a moment's hesitation, Dimitri's arms dropped away. Elle's body sagged and her lungs felt suddenly too tight to draw in a breath. Whatever she'd been expecting, a physical confrontation had never even entered her mind. She felt Dimitri's fingers poke into her back below her shoulder blades and her chest tightened even more as he nudged her away from his body in Kat's direction. *E tu, Brute?* She choked back a sob. They were all against her. She'd been expecting it, but Dimitri had seemed so certain…she'd thought he…she'd been a fool to believe…

What little breath she'd been able to suck in left Elle's body in a shocked whoosh as Kat grabbed her and pulled her into a suffocating hug. So maybe the *Earthbound* Archangel witch planned to use her supernatural powers to simply crush the life out of her?

When Kat drew back at last, Elle's arms still hung limply at her sides. She opened and closed her mouth, but couldn't seem to get a word out.

"Look, Kassian," Kat laughed, "Elle is totally speechless."

"And people say there are no miracles left in the world," McAllister drawled in a dry voice.

"But I don't understand…what I am…what I've done…I thought you would be so hurt, so angry…and that whole lightshow…"

"The lightshow, as you call it, was my empath reacting to your memories. I still can't control the whole Archangel part very well…but if I had John Gatewick in front of me right now, I'm pretty sure I could fry him like a pork rind without a second thought." Kat frowned. "As for being hurt and angry. I am. I'm hurt that you didn't trust our friendship enough to tell me the truth sooner. I'm angry that you would run away rather than tell me now, believing I would hold your past against you when it was never your fault. For a bright woman, you really are a complete and total idiot! Your father may have taught you to shield your thoughts, but I'm also an empath, you dipshit. Did you really think I wouldn't know there was more to your story than what you told me?"

"He's not my father."

"Maybe not, maybe so. Doesn't matter. Can't pick your relatives."

"So even knowing something was off, you took me in … and when they came looking, you protected me, lied for me, even knowing I used you?" Elle shook her head in stunned disbelief.

"You were desperate, I was lonely." Kat shrugged.

101

"So I guess in a way I used you as much as you used me. Besides, I could feel those guys coming a mile away. They were evil, you weren't. I wouldn't have given anyone up to those sleezebags. I took a chance and it paid off in the end."

"Did it? Seems like this is a hell of a way to repay you. I should have trusted you. I should have told you everything years ago. I just didn't know how. I'm so sorry, Kat." Elle croaked. Her throat ached with unshed tears. She'd been prepared for anger and recrimination. She hadn't expected embraces and rational conversation. She couldn't decide on an appropriate reaction.

"Yeah, you should have," Kat agreed without hesitation. "But you were desperate and scared, and I guess I can understand why you didn't feel like you could tell me back then. But now? I thought we were way past that! I told you about Kassian, and the *Earthbound*, my parents, and Luca, and well, everything…even when some people thought it was the worst idea in the world." She paused to shoot a dark look in her husband's direction. "Yet you still chose to run rather than level with me. I won't lie, Elle. It cuts pretty deep."

"I know. I'm sorry," Elle repeated in a whisper. "I really don't know what else to say. I realize it doesn't change anything, but I thought I was protecting you." When Kat raised her brows in clear disbelief, Elle hurried on. "I thought he might try to get to me through you… but you're right." She flicked a glance in McAllister's direction. "I knew your husband would never let them get near you. The truth is, I didn't want to face you, didn't want to deal with your rejection when you learned the truth about me. I took the coward's way out. It was a selfish decision and you deserved better."

"Won't get any arguments from me."

Elle took a deep breath and nodded. "I wish I had a do-over, Kat. But I don't. I can only tell you again that I'm sorry. I know there isn't any way to make it up to you, but…"

"Hmmm." Kat tapped a long, manicured nail against her chin. "Maybe there is."

"What?" Elle, Dimitri, and McAllister exclaimed in unison.

"The black Louboutin ankle boots." Kat narrowed her eyes and her lips curled in an evil grin. "You've got 'em, I want 'em."

Elle's mouth fell open. The single pair of shoes Elle loved more than any other she'd ever owned? Her Louboutins with the crisscrossed laces, open toes, and sensually curved heels? The shoes made of leather so supple it made butter look tough? Those boots brought sexy and edgy to a whole new level and were the one designer indulgence she'd been unable to leave behind, even when she'd downsized at the hotel. They were right at this moment lovingly wrapped in acid free tissue and stuffed in the bottom of the bag sitting at Dimitri's feet. *Those* black Louboutin ankle boots?

"Katrina, don't be ridiculous!" McAllister groused. "I'll buy you a hundred pairs of boots if you want them."

"Of course you will," Kat replied levelly, her eyes never leaving Elle's. "But that requires absolutely no sacrifice on Elle's part, does it? Is my forgiveness worth more to her than her favorite shoes, I wonder?"

Elle swallowed the urge to laugh and bit into her lower lip, hard, to keep from smiling. It was going to be all right. Unbelievably, Kat had forgiven her and their friendship remained intact. It was a gift she knew she didn't deserve, and she locked it away in her heart and treasured it accordingly.

"Can I borrow them, sometimes?"

"Perhaps," Kat replied airily.

"The price of your forgiveness is high, *Kemosabe*. Still, I guess you're worth it. Deal."

Elle stuck out her hand and Kat shook it solemnly before tugging Elle into her arms. They pulled apart wiping at their eyes, simultaneously laughing and crying while the men looked on in confusion.

"I mean it's not like you can ever *wear* them or anything. You'll never fit those enormous clown feet of yours into them no matter how much the leather stretches." Elle sniffed haughtily.

Kat linked her arm through Elle's and dragged her toward the door. "I'll have you know my large, but slender and beautifully pedicured toes are perfectly proportioned to my tall willowy frame. Thank heavens I am not a small, stunted troll with size six tootsies like some people I know."

"I believe the description you're struggling so hard to avoid is delicately petite. Jealousy will get you everywhere."

They'd nearly reached the door to the stairs leading down to the McAllister penthouse when Kat paused and they both looked over their shoulders at the two men staring at them like they were aliens who'd dropped out of the sky.

"Coming? I mean, I know we're good but I don't

think we can figure out how to take Gatewick and his operation down all by ourselves."

Dimitri exchanged a look with Mac before bending down to grab Elle's bag, gratified to see his fellow warrior looked equally befuddled by the exchange that had just taken place. Against all odds, and one coveted pair of boots later, it appeared the drama was over with limited tears and without a drop of blood being shed in the process. *So* not the kind of confrontations he was used to. Shaking his head, he followed Mac through the doorway into which Kat and Elle had already disappeared. If he lived another seven hundred years, Dimitri decided he would never understand women.

Chapter Eleven

"I suspect he created me using a DNA microinjection technique. Though from what little I could learn about his work, Gatewick seemed to focus primarily on Retroviruses. But with a Retrovirus-mediated gene transfer technique, he would have had to inbreed for twenty or more generations to achieve his goal. DNA microinjection has a low rate of success, but it's a one and done deal as far as producing an offspring with a homozygous genome...yeah, I guess that would be me. Ta-freakin'-da," Elle pronounced with more than a hint of sarcasm.

Dimitri chugged down his last swig of beer and set the empty bottle on the glass-topped coffee table with a plunk. He slouched in one black leather armchair and Elle perched on the edge of the other while the McAllisters sat hip to hip on the large matching sofa. He bit back a grin at the look on the faces of Mac and Kat McAllister as they stared at Elle in utter confusion. He supposed Mac would have to retract his earlier opinion that the woman had nothing in her head but the latest shoe sale. Damn, he loved a woman with a brain. *Loved?* Well, sure, he *cared* about her, and he wanted her maybe more than air to breathe, but *love*? Wow, where in the hell had *that* come from?

No one responded and the McAllisters simply continued to gape.

Elle flushed and twisted her fingers together in her lap, but continued. "Based on my initial research, I worried I might be transgenic, but upon further consideration, I think maybe I could be more accurately classified as cysgenic?"

She glanced at Dimitri and he nodded.

"Transgenic offspring result from the genetic material from one species being added to the genetic material of another unrelated species. But if the genetic material used is from the same species or a species that can naturally breed with the host, the result is a cysgenic organism. While humans and *Earthbound* are *technically* different species, they *can* mate and produce offspring," he confirmed.

"But why?" Kat shook her head and seemed to come out of the academia induced stupor. "What's the bottom line in the whole thing? So, Gatewick does a little genetic modification combined with in vitro fertilization and successfully produces a child with *Earthbound* DNA. What does he gain?"

"Elle thinks he's trying to build a better human, one with *Earthbound* longevity and accelerated healing ability." Dimitri snagged another beer and settled back into the deep leather upholstery. "Just between us, I'm a little concerned he might be on the right track. You all assumed Luca's awesome skill was the reason Elle survived his dagger to her chest. Fiorelli and I have had each other's backs on more occasions than I care to recall, and he's better with a knife than anyone I know, but let's face it, he was a little distracted by Callista at the time. Considering the distance and the size of the target, he made an amazing attempt, but it wasn't perfect. He nicked Elle's aorta. Technically, she should have bled out long before I got in there."

Elle gasped and the color drained from her face. Dimitri scrubbed a hand over his jaw and looked away from the accusatory glare of those big, blue eyes clearly saying he could have mentioned her unusual recovery a little sooner. *And* a little more privately. Dimitri exhaled on a long sigh. Sometimes he was about as subtle as a baseball bat to the head. He guessed he needed to work on that.

"So you're saying…?" Mac left the question dangling in the air.

"I'm saying that Elle *does* exhibit some evidence of accelerated healing abilities. Luca's aim was slightly off and given the resulting injury, she should be dead."

Kat disentangled herself from her husband and jumped to her feet. Perching on the arm of Elle's chair, she reached for her friend's hand and griped it tightly.

"But thanks to Dimitri, you aren't dead, so don't even go there," she admonished.

Elle shook her head slowly, her gaze fixed on Dimitri. He shifted uncomfortably. He'd been baffled by her survival from the beginning, knowing he couldn't take the credit for it no matter how developed his medical skills. Once he learned the truth about her origins, it all fell into place. And judging by the look in her eyes, it had all just clicked for Elle, too.

"Thanks to Dimitri, I had wonderful, compassionate care," Elle agreed in a pained voice that cut Dimitri to his soul. "But *you* didn't actually save me did you, Big Guy? I saved myself. Maybe you could write me up for one of your medical journals, huh? Arabella Penelope Gatewick, Test Tube Angel."

Dimitri leaned forward, propping his elbows on his

knees and lacing his fingers together. He looked directly into her eyes across the length of the coffee table as if they were the only two people in the room. Her shields held firm, but even without the benefit of telepathy, or Kat's empathic talents, he knew her well enough by now to understand she'd reverted to feeling like a freakish experiment.

"I am going to say this one more time. I can't force you to believe me. Okay, actually I can since *Earthbound* are able to manipulate minds to a degree, but I would never do that to you. Baby, you are smart and beautiful and uniquely you. You're strong and resourceful, maybe a little quirky and insecure, but hey, we all have our issues. I won't even pretend to understand the shoe fetish, as I myself own just three pair, two of which are motorcycle boots. It doesn't make any difference to me or to anyone here if you were conceived in a petri dish, a seedy motel, or the back of a fifty-seven Chevy. How you started your life is a minute and insignificant footnote in the story of who you are. When I look into your eyes, Arabella Penelope Gatewick..." Dimitri bit back a grin. "Okay, sorry, can't really get past the Penelope..." Elle's attention was riveted on him and she never even blinked.

"When I look in your eyes," he cleared his throat uncomfortably aware he had apparently suffered a psychotic break and was pretty much laying his heart on the table with an audience and no certainty of how Elle would respond. Hell, he'd been fighting it for weeks and it was probably about time he acknowledged he'd lost the battle. He'd just never foreseen he'd be waving the white flag in public. But she needed this.

Not later when they were alone, not tomorrow, not next week. Now. She needed validation she was *someone* instead of *something*. If he made an ass of himself, so be it. It's not like it would be a novel experience. Somehow, though these weeks with her hadn't completely appeased his fear of binding his soul to a mortal woman with a finite lifespan, he'd mostly replaced it with the quiet realization that at least a broken heart would mean he'd allowed himself to love someone deeply enough for it to break. And that love, however long it lasted, was worth it. She was worth it. He didn't know how many years they would have, but maybe it was okay to be uncertain. They could be uncertain together and maybe it would help them appreciate each day they did share. "When I look in your eyes I don't see test tubes or petri dishes or laboratories. I don't see DNA or irrelevant genetic composition. When I look in your eyes, I see what no science can create or replicate. I see the radiance of your soul. I see you."

When he finished speaking, Dimitri closed his eyes and dropped his forehead onto his clasped hands. In the profound silence that followed, he swore he heard the dust settling on the furniture. Elle's reaction, when it came at last, originated completely from left field and her voice was much closer than he expected.

"What do you mean you can't get past the Penelope? Did you know the original Penelope faithfully waited twenty years for her husband Odysseus to return from the Trojan War? And it's not like she didn't have offers, Dimitri. Lots of them. I'm quite taken with the name, really."

Dimitri opened his eyes and glimpsed the toes of

Elle's shoes planted directly in front of his. He raised his head slowly, drinking in every inch of her, feet shoulder width apart, fists planted on shapely hips, lips pressed in a thin line, and brows arched sharply over blue, blue eyes glinting with moisture and doubt.

"Seriously? I spill my guts in a room full of people and that's what you take away from it?"

"Kat and Kassian hardly constitute a room full of people. You're going to have to own the Penelope, Dimitri."

What the hell, it was just a name, wasn't it? Dimitri turned it over and over in his mind. He sat back in the chair and looked up at her, standing in front of him, taut as a bowstring, waiting. Kat remained on the arm of the chair Elle had vacated, smiling against the fingers pressed to her lips. Mac drummed his fingertips on the arm of the sofa, head turned in the direction of the wall of windows overlooking the city. The seconds ticked by and Dimitri knew his response to this seemingly innocuous issue was vitally important. Elle shifted from one foot to the other and a flash of uncertainty crossed her face. Like a ray of sunlight piercing a bank of storm clouds, it hit him. It might not make sense to anyone else, but he got it. She needed him to accept the name, before she could truly believe he accepted everything else about her. And if he could accept her completely, she could completely accept herself.

"Well, I guess if you can live with my scarred mug, I can live with Penelope."

"What scars?"

His grin cramped his cheeks. He reached out and grabbed the waistband of her jeans, tugging until she tumbled awkwardly into his lap and settled against his chest right over his painfully thumping heart.

"Did you know that when the Japanese mend something that's been broken, they fill the cracks with gold? They believe when something's been damaged it has a history and that makes it even more valuable, more beautiful. I read it on the internet so it must be true, right?" She traced her finger lightly along the length of his scar and smiled into his eyes. For a heartbeat, he found himself lost in their blue depths. He realized at that moment when he looked into her eyes he didn't simply see *her*, he saw the missing part of himself. Whether she was human or *Earthbound* or some unknown species in between, she was his.

"Seriously?" he asked.

"Seriously."

"Okay, then." He lifted her slightly, removing her firm, wiggling backside from his now aching groin, and settled her more comfortably on his thigh. Her lips curved up with a knowing smile, but she made no comment and simply snuggled into him like a contented kitten. "Now where were we?"

"Before or after Cupid and his army of cherubs swooped in with little golden arrows?" Mac responded dryly, crooking a finger at his wife to call her back to his side.

"Before." Dimitri shot back placidly, completely immune to his friend's obvious sarcasm. He well remembered the lump of putty his brother warrior had been in Kat's hands when they first hooked up.

"I believe we were discussing the finer points of genetic engineering, though when all is said and done, the how is far less important than the why. Wouldn't you agree?" Mac arched a brow.

"Absolutely. Thoughts?"

"Kassian, does Cupid really have an army of little cherubs?" Kat playfully poked her husband in the chest.

"Cupid is a foolish, flighty little boy who likes to give himself far more credit than he's due. Now can we please get back to the problem at hand?"

"Elle thinks Gatewick might be working with the *Librarians* in an attempt to create some sort of super-race," Dimitri offered. "For what ultimate purpose, who knows, but consider a suicide bomber who doesn't die and could be recycled for multiple missions. That would be a pretty valuable commodity, don't you think?"

"But, why continue playing with the Retrovirus-mediated gene transfer if he'd had success with DNA microinjection?" Elle mused aloud. "That's always bothered me. If his goal is to create his own version of *Earthbound*, why not stick with a method that's proven successful?"

"Well, you said yourself a lot of this is based on supposition on your part. You don't really know for sure what technique he used or even what he's really up to, right?" Kat pointed out.

"Yeah, I guess so. It just seemed to be the theory that made the most sense," Elle conceded with a sigh.

Mac glanced down at his wife, who shrugged before they both looked directly at Dimitri.

"How many more bombshells do you think she can absorb tonight?" Dimitri heard Mac's voice in his head on the common channel used by all *Earthbound*.

"She's pretty tough. Why?" Dimitri narrowed his eyes at his friends.

"She has a right to know all of it, Kassian," Kat

113

interjected. *"Look at everything I had thrown at me in a short period of time. I coped. I know Elle and she will, too."*

"Dimitri?" Mac gave Dimitri the call, acknowledging the bond between his brother *Defensori* and his wife's best friend.

Dimitri told Elle he believed she was strong and resourceful and he did. Whatever came, she would deal with it. And if her own strength failed her, she could borrow on his. That's the way this love stuff worked, right? Yeah, he loved her. He could admit it to himself now, and accept it. He waited for the panic to hit, but it never came. Feeling as though he'd lived the last several hundred years looking at his life through an impenetrable fog, in this moment he had total clarity, and what he saw beyond the mist was Elle. He loved her and he had to learn to live in the present and let the future worry about itself.

"What are you three talking about?" Elle pouted.

"You *heard* that?" Dimitri pulled back and looked at her incredulously.

"Not really," Elle's face wrinkled in concentration. "More like a buzzing sensation in my head and a feeling I was missing something. And I know you guys have that whole telepathy thing going on."

Dimitri exchanged a worried glance with Mac. Maybe Gatewick had been more successful than any of them imagined. Was it possible that because Elle's *Earthbound* was genetically engineered, it simply took time for her powers to develop rather than them being present from birth? Mac shrugged and shook his head. They were all navigating new territory and clearly Mac had no more insight into the possibilities than Dimitri.

"Elle," Kat began slowly. "What did Gatewick tell you about the *Librarians*?"

Elle sat up straighter in his lap, accidentally grinding her bottom into his crotch. When she turned to grin at him, he realized it was no accident and that sent his blood racing in a way that made an uncomfortable situation even worse.

"He said they were a secret society whose mission was to observe and record *Earthbound* activity and do whatever it took to prevent them from interfering with human history," she replied.

"Here's the thing, Elle," Mac began slowly. "Gatewick lied."

Shifting her position, Elle draped an arm over the back of the chair, and began to twirl a lock of Dimitri's hair nervously around her finger. It was as sensuously silky as she'd imagined it would be. He loved her. Oh, he hadn't said the words, and neither had she, but it was there in the air between them and they'd get around to it eventually. It was enough for now he'd made it clear he accepted her, every part of her. Knowing he still wanted her with all of her truths exposed and her secrets laid bare gave her a peace she'd never known and hadn't even been aware she craved until now. She felt as though she could cope with anything McAllister threw at her as long as she had Dimitri at her side. Of course, if he ever called her Penelope, she might have to kill him.

Chapter Twelve

"Gatewick lied? Well, call the press 'cause there's a newsflash," Elle's lips twisted into a grimace as she leaned back against Dimitri's chest now that she felt the freedom to do so. His arms tightened around her imperceptibly, giving her the unasked for support he always seemed able to anticipate. "C'mon, McAllister. I know you're dying to spit it out. Let me have it."

Instead of continuing, McAllister drew in a deep breath and released it through pursed lips, while his wife favored him with an expectant smile.

"Yes, by all means, McAllister. Spit it out. It won't kill you, I promise."

"Fine. Elle, whatever impression you may have gotten, I do not dislike you. I freely admit, I completely misjudged you and totally underestimated you and, for whatever it's worth, I apologize." He frowned down at Katrina. "Happy, Wife?"

"You know what they say, McAllister. Happy wife, happy life. You may continue." She waggled her brows in Elle's direction. Elle simply shook her head affectionately at her friend knowing she had coerced the apology from the dark, frowning man at her side.

"You know, McAllister, if you weren't wearing such a painfully constipated expression during the delivery, I might perceive that apology as a little more sincere. Admit it, you bought the ditzy shopaholic act of mine hook, line, and Louboutins. Guess that makes you the bigger airhead, huh?"

"Pushing." Mac ground out between clenched teeth when Elle continued to grin and Katrina actually had the audacity to giggle. "I said it and I meant it, okay? Can we move on now?"

"By all means. Apology accepted, by the way." Elle knew Kat had instigated the apology and for Kat's sake, she would give McAllister's sincerity the benefit of the doubt. But really, did he have to look as though he was having his teeth pulled?

"Good. Anyway, the *Librarians* have been around for thousands of years, and part of what Gatewick told you *is* true. Their mission, as they see it, is to observe and record *Earthbound* history. Period. They don't interfere with us and we don't interfere with them. My brother Alec, however, has managed to cultivate a couple of friendships within the organization that have been mutually beneficial, and he utilizes their research facilities from time to time."

"So he's the brains and you're the brawn?"

"I'm going to ignore that."

"As you wish. Pray continue."

"When I filled Alec in earlier, he made a couple of calls. The *Librarians* categorically deny any affiliation with John Gatewick or his research."

"I don't understand," Elle untangled her fingers from Dimitri's hair and sat up straighter. "Why would he want people to believe he was a member? Seems like an odd thing to lie about."

"I don't know," McAllister admitted. "The most plausible explanation either Alec or I can come up with is that whatever his ultimate goal, he wants to somehow pin any potential fallout on the *Librarians* by perpetuating the idea he's working under their patronage. Maybe he's holding some kind of grudge."

Elle jumped to her feet, strode across the room, and began to pace the width of the floor to ceiling windows overlooking the city, one arm wrapped around her waist and the other tapping out the rhythm of her steps against her thigh.

"Baby, what are you doing?" Dimitri asked.

"Writing."

"Excuse me?"

"I'm writing. In my head, I mean. I'm trying to look at all of this as though it's the plot in a novel and hypothesize a logical conclusion. Can't hurt, right?"

"Actually," McAllister sat forward and his brows flew into his hairline. "With your talent, that might be the most productive idea I've heard all night."

Elle arched a brow. "I think that's the nicest thing you've ever said to me, McAllister."

"Savor it," he advised with a grin.

"See, Kassian," Kat rose gracefully to her feet and patted her husband on the head. "You said something nice about Elle all by yourself and it didn't even kill you. Coffee, anyone?"

"I'll deal with you later, wife," McAllister swatted his wife's behind as she headed off in the direction of the kitchen.

"I'm counting on it, husband," she laughed over her shoulder.

"I still don't get it. How do the *Fallen* figure into all this?" McAllister directed the question at Elle. "I can't see any reason they'd back any project with the potential to increase the number of *Earthbound* on the planet."

"No idea." Elle shrugged. "In fact, until Dimitri mentioned them, I never even suspected they were involved. Sure, there were always others around, but I couldn't tell you if they were human, *Earthbound*, or *Fallen*. Oh, and Gatewick has a backer, Justin Chen. Gatewick sure as hell doesn't have the means to finance this sort of thing on his own."

"Name Chen ring a bell?" McAllister asked.

"Nope." Dimitri shook his head slowly.

"Maybe it's just a coincidence and the *animorti* really were tracking Dimitri?" Elle asked hopefully.

"Unlikely. Don't forget Kat's recollection of the men who came looking for you after you escaped. She knew they were evil, though she probably attributed the knowledge to her empathic abilities at the time. Probably *animorti*. I think we have to assume that whatever Gatewick's agenda, a *Fallen* is behind it at worst or integrally involved at best."

A gray curtain obscured her vision and Elle felt her bones dissolve as her mind went to a place she fought hard to keep it from traveling. A pair of strong arms caught her as she felt herself crumple to the floor, and pulled her securely against a solid, broad chest. She blinked rapidly into Dimitri's worried face and her breath came in uneven little pants as she struggled to clear her vision and hold onto consciousness.

"What the hell…" McAllister muttered as Dimitri strode to the sofa and McAllister shot to his feet to make room.

"Get those pillows under her legs," Dimitri instructed briskly as he lowered her carefully to the couch, his voice sounding faint and faraway. McAllister grasped both her ankles in one large hand and raised her legs as though they weighed nothing while stuffing a mound of decorative cushions beneath them. Dimitri crouched next to the sofa, tenderly brushing her hair back from her forehead. "What is it, baby? What happened?"

Elle concentrated on Dimitri's beautiful dark eyes gazing down at her with such concern, and willed the mist to clear. Her fingers tangled in the neck of his T-shirt, fisting the fabric like a lifeline. Pleading with her eyes, she opened her mouth to speak but her still racing pulse fluttered like the wings of a hundred moths in her throat, stealing her breath and leaving her gasping.

"Breathe with me, honey. C'mon, watch me…like this…smell a rose, blow out a candle." Elle concentrated on mimicking Dimitri, pulling in great gulps of air through her nose and blowing it out through tightly pursed lips until the fluttering subsided and she resumed breathing almost normally. She still held his shirt in a stranglehold and pulled him to her when he made a move to sit back on his heels.

"What if I'm one of *them*?" She whispered in a choked voice.

"What? Who?" Dimitri's dark brows knit together in a genuinely puzzled expression. With a groan, Elle released his shirt and struggled to raise herself onto her elbows. His arm went immediately under her shoulders to assist her into a sitting position and McAllister pulled a couple of the pillows out from under her legs and shoved them behind her back. Elle pushed her hair back off of her face with a shaky hand and drew in a deep breath.

"If *Fallen* are behind this, what if my DNA isn't

Earthbound at all. What if…what if my DNA is actually *Fallen*? It isn't like Gatewick didn't lie about everything else. Oh God, Dimitri…what if I'm one of *them*?"

Elle buried her face in her hands. What if, after everything—escaping Gatewick's compound, building a life, exposing her secrets, and finding the man she suspected was her once in a lifetime—it turned out she was biologically his sworn enemy, the product of evil?

"Oh my God, Elle! What happened?" Katrina's shriek was followed by the clatter of a serving tray and its contents as she dropped it on the coffee table.

"C'mon, Kat. She's okay. Let's give them a minute, huh?" McAllister's quiet directive was accompanied by the sound of reluctant footsteps and followed by the decisive click of a door.

"Elle, look at me." Dimitri's fingers gently tugged hers away from her face when she made no move to obey, and he kept her hands firmly in his. "You aren't. It isn't possible."

"Of course it is! What if Gatewick used DNA taken from a *Fallen* instead of an *Earthbound?* That makes me a *Fallen*, duh!"

"Move over, my legs are going numb in this position. I'm not as young as I used to be." Dimitri straightened to his full height and stretched as Elle shifted and tossed some of the pillows to the floor. Then he dropped down beside her and pulled her against him, tucking her under his shoulder so the side of her face rested directly over his heart.

"I promise you aren't a *Fallen*. If sharing some DNA was the deciding factor then everyone in this apartment would be in deep shit."

"You're just saying that to make me feel better," Elle sniffed miserably. Dimitri's chest rumbled against her cheek.

"Well, I guess after seeing you turn gray and nearly keel over I probably *would* say that to make you feel better," he chuckled. "But, I promise you're no more a *Fallen* than I am."

"I've never fainted in my life. Gah! I'm becoming a total wuss. And how do you know for sure?"

"You aren't a wuss. You're overwhelmed. Now, let me see if I can explain the whole *Fallen* thing." He pressed his lips to the top of her head, and she snuggled against him, wrapping her arms around his solid middle and hanging on for dear life, wanting so desperately to believe him.

"I'm sure you already know the *Fallen* were cast out of the heavens and damned for sedition and disobedience?" Elle nodded against his chest. "And how after the *Fall*, one faction of the rebels quickly realized they'd gotten caught up in a deliberately misleading political scheme and sought forgiveness and reconciliation?" She nodded again. "To make a long story short, *Earthbound* and *Fallen* share a common history up to a point, and thus a common biology. Bottom line is, we share very similar DNA, and which side of the divide we find ourselves on isn't determined by biology. Believe me, baby. No matter who provided your DNA, you don't have to worry about which side you're on."

"You're sure?"

"I'd stake my soul on it. Trust me. The sensations creeping up my spine when I'm around you have nothing to do with evil. Okay?"

A sense of relief that left her as limp as a wet noodle snaked through her. She took a deep cleansing breath and pushed away from Dimitri's chest. Tilting her head back, she looked into his eyes and saw all the acceptance and reassurance she would ever need.

"Okay."

His gaze roamed over her face as though he needed to convince himself she was all right. Elle reached up, curled her fingers around the nape of his neck, and pulled his head down. When his lips closed over hers, Elle feared she might drown in the sheer physical pleasure of him. She nearly groaned aloud when he buried his fingers in her hair and cupped the back of her head, pulling her closer and deepening the kiss. His warm tongue teased along the crease in her lips and she opened for him without hesitation. He swept inside, seeking, stroking, plundering, as if he couldn't get enough of the kiss, enough of her. His other hand stroked down her back and splayed across her buttocks, hitching her more tightly against him. Elle lost all sense of time and place, her mind temporarily emptied of everything except Dimitri and the desire exploding low in her gut. She slipped a hand under his T-shirt and skimmed her palm over the rock hardness of his stomach. His muscles twitched in response. As her seeking fingers, with a mind of their own, began moving lower, he snatched her hand, and with a growl that should have had teeth, brought it to his chest where he held it trapped beneath his and tore his lips from hers. His heart hammered against her palm in the same frantic dance taking place in her own chest. She raised questioning eyes to his and saw passion and frustration clouding his gaze. His breathing as harsh and ragged as hers, he dropped a chaste kiss on the top of her head, and let his own fall back against the sofa with a sigh.

"By all means, join us," he croaked. "It's your living room, after all."

"Nice of you to remember."

Elle's cheeks warmed as Kat and her comically grinning husband strolled back into the room hand in hand. Her face grew even hotter when Kat winked and rolled her eyes in Dimitri's direction. What on earth was wrong with her? She'd schooled herself years ago to never get so caught up in anything that she became blinded to everything else around her. She'd never had the luxury of letting down her guard so completely, always aware she lived in a house of cards that could collapse around her at any moment.

"You're a bad influence, Radchenko," she grumbled into his shoulder.

"You started it," he replied, keeping his eyes closed, but allowing the corners of his lips to curve up.

"Well, you didn't exactly beat me off with a stick."

"Haven't slept in two days. I figured I lacked the strength."

"Hey! Speaking of sleeping…my nightmare…I didn't have it last night!"

"I know."

"You know?"

"Yep. I was there, remember?" Dimitri opened his eyes and picked up his head to look over at McAllister. "Alec's here."

Kat hurried to the door and threw it open. Then she launched herself into the open arms of an extremely attractive dark-haired man with laughing blue eyes.

"Your wife is inordinately happy to see me, Kass,"

Alec McAllister laughed, stepping into the room and dropping his bag inside the door while keeping an arm around his sister-in-law.

"For reasons I will never understand, she likes you. She really likes you." McAllister stepped forward and briefly embraced his brother, pounded him soundly on the back, and tugged Kat along with him when he stepped away. "It's good to see you, Alec."

"You, too." He stepped aside to reveal another man behind him. The guy was huge, bigger even than Dimitri. A bald giant with ear gauges the size of nickels and Japanese throwing stars tattooed all over his scalp. His black tee strained across a chest nearly as wide as the doorway. His eyes scanned the room. He nodded to Dimitri and fixed his gaze on Elle. Her stomach flipped. And then he smiled. He had a beautiful smile, and with his shockingly green eyes twinkling in amusement, he wasn't quite as intimidating as she first thought. "So, I hear we've got a microchip to scan?"

Chapter Thirteen

Galen passed the handheld scanner over Elle's wrist for the fourth time, glanced again at the laptop screen with a frown, then shook his head and clicked off the scanner.

"Typical RFID transponder. Doesn't tell us a thing." He blew out a deep breath and rose to his feet. He snapped his laptop shut and shoved it, and the scanner, back into his bag.

"Maybe you could dummy that down for those of us who don't spend our evenings with our nose buried in the latest Technology Today," McAllister muttered. "What the hell is RFID?"

"RFID, or Radio-frequency identification, is a wireless use of radio-frequency electromagnetic fields to transfer data," Galen laughed, dropping into a chair and reaching for one of the beers Kat had just carried in from the kitchen. "Thanks, gorgeous." He took a long draw from the bottle before continuing. "Lots of industrial uses…access management, tracking of product on assembly lines, that kind of thing. You might be more familiar with it in terms of toll collections. You know the little box your driver keeps on the dashboard so you can zip through the tollbooth without stopping to pay? Courtesy of RIFD."

"So there isn't any data on it?" Elle asked in a voice thick with disappointment. She'd been so hopeful

126

the microchip was the key to bringing Gatewick down.

"Oh there's data, but it could be something as simple as an ID number similar to those used by pet owners. Mary Jane's pampered pooch gets lost, shows up at a shelter, and the shelter scans for the microchip. The ID number coincides with the registration information provided by Mary Jane and Rover gets to go home. Yours could be linked to information in an external database somewhere, too. But there's no way of knowing what or where just from the chip itself."

"You don't think it could be some kind of tracking device do you?" Dimitri asked. "I'm more than a little concerned they managed to tail her to Katrina's house. Especially since *I* tailed her to Katrina's house and never noticed anyone or anything out of the ordinary."

"Well, there's nothing this size in GPS commercially available that I know of, but they're using RFID chips in passports these days so I guess anything's possible," Galen replied with a grin. "But even with passports, a high powered reader has to be within about a hundred and sixty feet to pick up the signal, so it's unlikely Elle could have been *located* by that method."

"But what if they knew where to look to begin with?" Elle's teeth worried at her bottom lip. "I don't remember much about what happened when Azakriel was in control, but it seems too coincidental Gatewick contacted me so soon after that when I'd managed to stay off of his radar for all these years. I've been assuming the demon contacted him and told him where I was. If he knew where to start looking, it wouldn't be all that hard to keep tabs on me, would it?"

"I guess not," Galen allowed. "But if that's the

case, why haven't they already grabbed you? The demon possessed you months ago, so if that's how Gatewick was alerted to your location, he's had ample opportunity. Yeah, Dimitri was hanging around, but it's not like he was there constantly or guarding you twenty-four-seven. Hell, until today, no one knew there was anything or anyone to guard you *from*. So why didn't Gatewick simply get you while the getting was good?"

"I don't know," Elle admitted. "But now that you mention it, why didn't he? Why didn't he just send someone to grab me? Even when I was at Kat's house, Nerd-nuts came to the door, but Dimitri said there were *Fallen* nearby to pick him up. Why send a human? They didn't know Dimitri was there. Heck, *I* didn't know Dimitri was there. Why not just grab me then?"

"No idea," Galen echoed Elle's sentiment. "There's one other possibility that comes to mind about the microchip, though. It could be security related."

"Like an access code," Dimitri pondered slowly.

"Exactly," Galen confirmed.

"So maybe he doesn't want me back at all. Maybe he never did." Elle whispered. She was surprised to realize that the fact her father considered her disposable still hurt in a place she didn't think existed anymore. She swallowed hard over the lump of sadness lodged behind her breastbone. Despite everything, he'd been kind to her in his own way. She'd even believed he loved her until she learned the truth. Enough! She refused to waste another breath or another tear wishing things could have been different. Gatewick wasn't worth it. She cleared her throat as the others regarded her with quiet concern. "I thought running would keep him from learning of your existence and keep you safe. I guess I'm an even bigger fool than I thought. Apparently, he's been watching me for weeks at the very least. Maybe he wasn't waiting for an opportunity to get me back. Maybe he's just keeping tabs on me to make sure I haven't figured out I have the means to get the *Defensori* into his compound and bring them down on his head."

"If he thinks I...*we* would let you anywhere near him, he's not playing with a full deck. And we hardly need a measly microchip to gain entry anywhere," Dimitri grumbled.

"Elle's very existence speaks to the fact he thought he could experiment with impunity. Makes me think he has the place more secured than we might be giving him credit for," McAllister observed thoughtfully.

"Elle," Kat suddenly straightened next to her husband on the sofa. "Do you remember the summer we decided to plant our own garden?"

"Kind of random there, girlfriend," Elle laughed.

"No, think about it. We ended up with so many tomatoes we didn't know what to do with them. We made our own salsa, remember? All that chopping and dicing?"

"Of my fingers, you mean!" Elle snorted. She glanced at Dimitri. "Hope you weren't holding out for a domestic goddess, Big Guy."

"Exactly!" Kat exclaimed. "You did an absolutely outstanding job of almost chopping a finger off! Took seven stitches to close it, then it got infected, and it took forever to heal even with antibiotics!"

"Don't remind me. That one-handed hair style I rocked for weeks was not my best look."

"How long ago?" Elle felt Dimitri tense against her back and his arm came around her waist to hold her steady as he shifted his position.

"About four years," Kat regarded him with wide eyes, which she then turned on Elle. "What if it wasn't the demon? What if Gatewick knew where you were all along, but simply didn't care if you came back because you were useless to him, nothing but a failed experiment?"

"So now I'm not just a freakish experiment, I'm a failed one?" Elle realized she could say it now with none of her previous self-loathing since Dimitri's acceptance, and that of the others, had allowed her runaway train to Pity Central to derail at the Suck-it-up-Station. Dimitri was right. She was really no different than any other child born by in vitro. Even if there'd been some genetic tinkering involved, medical researchers were doing the same thing all the time in an effort to counteract congenital defects and diseases, right? Right. She decided from now on she would spin it just that way and never look back.

"Well, of course you're a freak, honey, but you're *our* freak." Kat grinned. "But that's not my point. Don't you get it? Dimitri said you should have died from Luca's dagger, but you didn't. You exhibited accelerated healing *after* the demon attack, but not before. Something changed."

"And earlier she sensed we were having a telepathic conversation," McAllister interjected. "Okay, so she couldn't make out the words, but she's been around us before and that never happened."

Elle's mouth dropped open and she felt sure her chin was in danger of hitting the floor as the ramification sank in. The blood pounded in her ears as she gripped Dimitri's hand—hard—and stared at all the other occupants of the room who were suddenly grinning like idiots. Before she recovered enough brain cells to speak, Dimitri, who wore a look she knew must be similar to her own, spoke up.

"Are you implying Azakriel's possession sparked some latent *Earthbound* tendencies in her DNA and jumpstarted them? Is that even possible?" Dimitri gasped.

Kat leaned back against her husband with a sigh and rolled her eyes.

"You know the trouble with you guys? You were born *Earthbound* and always knew who you were and what you were capable of."

Mac stretched his legs out in front of him and leaned his head back against the couch, closing his eyes with a groan. Alec settled for hiding his grin behind his half empty beer bottle. Obviously, they'd both heard this particular spiel before.

"One would think given who and what you are, the question of the impossible would never even arise. One would be wrong. Clearly, those of us who came into our identity a little later in life have a much better grasp of the whole 'anything's possible' vibe."

A peculiar ache squeezed the center of Dimitri's chest and he found it hard to breathe as the iron cage he'd constructed to protect his heart from the pain of loss creaked and crumbled. Forged by the murder of his family and tempered by the loss of countless patients and friends over the long centuries of his life, the fortress he'd built failed completely in the face of an emotion he thought he could no longer feel—hope. Of course, only the passing of time could confirm it, but the possibility demonic possession had potentially increased Elle's longevity staggered him. It was more than he dared dream of when he reluctantly accepted what he felt for her was too deep to walk away from no matter what it cost him in the end.

"Dimitri?" Elle's voice sounded far away. "What's wrong with you? You look a little green."

"I…just realized. Maybe you aren't going to die soon after all."

The other three men were regarding Dimitri like a man who'd gone a little soft in the head. But not Katrina. A tremulous smile split her face from ear to ear. Clearly, her empath picked up on the churning emotion Dimitri knew he must have been throwing off faster than a menopausal woman shucking a wool sweater in July.

"Well, I kind of hoped your skills were up to the challenge of keeping me alive, Big Guy." Elle frowned.

"*Soon* is a relative term in *Earthbound* vernacular," Kat laughed, jumping up from the sofa and pulling her friend out of Dimitri's lap and into her arms. "I think what Dimitri is trying to say over that big lump in his throat is if you *are* developing *Earthbound* characteristics, you could live for a long time. A very long time. As in centuries."

Over Kat's shoulder, Elle's wide, shocked eyes locked on Dimitri. They'd deepened to the rich, dark blue of the sky before a storm. He couldn't help noticing she looked a little green around the gills herself at the moment. Something in his expression must have reassured her however, and the panicked look faded from her eyes. She hugged Kat back, extricated herself from her friend's embrace, and then came to stand between his knees. Looking down at him as though they were the only two people in the room, she reached to cup his jaw in her hand, rubbing her thumb lightly over his scar where it transected the angle of his cheekbone.

"If there's any way this is true…" she began in a hoarse voice, then paused and cleared her throat. "If this is true… I mean…the uh...listen, all that stuff you said before? I realize you weren't thinking in terms of my being here for damned near forever."

"I sure as hell wasn't," Dimitri confirmed without thinking, but her rapid blinking and the way her throat worked as she fought to hold her emotions in check told him that what he meant and what she understood were two entirely different things. He covered her hand with his and brought it to his lips. Never taking his eyes from hers, he grazed his lips along her knuckles before pressing a slow, firm kiss in the hollow of her palm. She curled her fingers inward as though she could catch and hold the sensation and a spark of desire lit her eyes through the glint of her tears. An answering heat curled low in his gut as he rose to his feet and buried his hands in the hair on either side of her head and tilted her face up to his.

"Baby, listen to me. I've lost too many people to count and believe me, it never hurts any less. Sometimes it feels like I've spent most of my life mourning someone. Life is a gift, but longevity? Yeah, sometimes it can feel like more of curse. I fought this thing between us with everything I had. The thought of binding my soul to yours and then losing you in a couple of decades? You're right, I wasn't thinking in terms of damn near forever. Because I believed forever with you was a gift I couldn't hope for."

"So let me get this straight," Elle whispered as a slow smile stretched her lips. "If it turns out you're stuck with me for longer than expected…you're on board with that?"

"Sweetness, I'm not just on board, I'm driving the freakin' boat." Dimitri grinned and hauled her hard against him, tasting her tears as his mouth locked on hers.

"Oh, for the love of…get a room," Mac groaned from the sofa. Dimitri thought it might have been the best suggestion he'd heard all night.

"And on that note, I think it's time for me to head out. I'm on patrol tonight," Galen tipped the last of his beer into his mouth and climbed to his feet. With little more than a pleasant nod, he stepped to the door, yanked it open, and disappeared.

"Not one for long good-byes is our Galen," Alec nodded in the direction of the door.

"You'll stay with us, of course?" Mac quirked a dark brow in his brother's direction.

"If it's not inconvenient," Alec responded. "I'll get my place opened up and aired out tomorrow if I decide to hang around a while."

"Well, I thought since we hadn't seen each other in ages Elle could stay with us in the guest room, so maybe Alec could take the couch?" Kat blinked up at Dimitri, her expression the picture of innocence. "I mean, she can't go back to her place, right? They could be watching it."

"I'm relatively sure they are," Dimitri replied without changing expression. "That won't be an issue however, since she'll be staying with me."

"Hey, look at me over here," Elle waved a hand in his face. "Last time I checked I was still able to speak for myself."

Dimitri released her, stepped back, and crossed his arms over his massive chest. Kat bit back a grin. Alec reached for another beer, and Elle thought McAllister couldn't have looked less interested if he tried.

"Well?" Dimitri arched a brow. Elle struggled to maintain a straight face. She found it totally endearing the way he stood there struggling to look as if her decision didn't matter to him one way or the other. She couldn't believe the big lug still had any doubts about where she would choose to spend the night no matter how much she'd missed Kat. She crossed the room to Kat and pulled her close for a quick hug.

"I'll talk to you tomorrow, m'kay?" She stepped back and turned to regard Kat's husband and his expression made stifling the urge to laugh a challenge. "You don't have to look so damned relieved, McAllister."

"Don't know what you're talking about," he protested. "You're more than welcome to stay in the guest room. To know my wife will finally have a good night's sleep after worrying about you all these weeks, I'll even fluff your damn pillows for you and make you a glass of warm milk."

"I appreciate the offer, but I think I'll take a rain check," Elle laughed. "Besides, I'm not sure Alec will actually *fit* on the sofa." Tall, broad, and well-muscled, Alec was at least as large as his warrior brother and nearly as big as Dimitri. With a mass of thick, dark curls, piercing blue eyes, and deep dimples when he smiled as he was doing now, she bet he'd left an army of women panting after him over the centuries. She'd have to be blind not to notice Alec McAllister was an exceptionally beautiful man. Curiously, while she could admire his looks, she didn't feel even a twinge of physical attraction.

"You're probably right about that. Of course the guestroom has a king-sized bed and there'd be plenty of room for both of us," Alec winked.

Elle's head whipped around in surprise at a sound that should have had claws rumbling up from Dimitri's chest. He quickly recovered, clearing his throat and schooling his features into a placid expression. Alec McAllister and his brother both burst out laughing.

"I don't think Dimitri appreciates your generosity, Alec," McAllister guffawed.

"Are you ready?" Dimitri growled, arching a brow in Elle's direction, his tone belying the indifferent look on his face. Elle swallowed a giggle of her own and nodded, reaching for his hand and lacing her fingers with his.

"Let me call you a car, bro," McAllister unfolded his long length from the sofa, still chuckling.

"Too risky. Your 'copter had your corporate emblem all over it. Anyone watching will have figured out exactly where we were headed and probably have eyes on the building as we speak. On the other hand, I doubt they have any idea where I live. We'll fade out from the hallway. Safer that way."

"Dimitri, you know I can't…" Elle began in a whisper. He simply squeezed her hand.

"Good thinking," McAllister nodded. "We'll touch base tomorrow and figure out what to do next. I know you were scheduled to back-up Galen tonight but I'll give him a call and tell him to alert me instead of you if he runs into trouble. You take a night off. It's been a hell of a long day for both of you."

"Sounds like a plan." Dimitri tugged Elle along with him as he headed in the direction of the door, bending to snag her bag from the floor near the entrance.

"Elle!" Katrina called suddenly and started in their direction. "You forgot something!"

Elle turned to her friend with a confused frown. "What?"

"The boots, girlfriend. Fork 'em over, a deal's a deal."

Chapter Fourteen

"I can't believe she actually took them," Elle pouted when the door to the McAllister apartment closed behind them and she and Dimitri stood alone in the dimly lit hallway.

"So you're telling me a pair of shoes is more important than a friendship?" Dimitri tipped her chin up with a forefinger and looked into her eyes, an amused glint flashing in his own deep brown ones. A reluctant grin tugged at the corners of Elle's lips.

"Of course not. It isn't really about the shoes anyway," Elle admitted. "Don't get me wrong, I love those booties, but it's really more about what they represent. When I left, I left everything behind. I kept the Louboutins to remind me that whatever my future might hold, I *had* been able to escape Gatewick and build a life. I *had* been successful. Successful enough to buy three thousand dollar shoes. I really do love my shoes, Dimitri. You probably think it's silly."

"No, I don't think it's silly. Okay, maybe a little silly. I've never understood women's obsession with shoes, but I think you'd do better to judge your success by the amazing woman you've become, the things you've accomplished, and the people who love you rather than by the things you own."

Elle considered that for a moment. At the time, the shoes had seemed so important, but what if Dimitri

138

hadn't stopped her from running? If she'd found herself starting over, alone in a strange place with strange people, after a while, would the iconic shoes really have meant anything without the people she loved?

"How did you get to be so smart?" She grinned up at him.

"Been around a while." He shrugged his massive shoulders and clamped his hands on her shoulders. "You ready to go?"

"I guess so," Elle couldn't control the nervous tremor in her voice. "But, how is this going to work?"

"I'm going to fade both of us to my place. Just hang on to me and it'll be over before you know it. Might wanna close your eyes though…it's likely to be a little disorienting the first time."

The *first* time? She sure hoped they weren't going to make a habit of this.

"You know, I'm really more of a limousine and public transportation kind of girl."

Without giving herself time to formulate another thought, she plastered her body to his, locking her hands together around his waist, squeezing her eyes closed, and burying her face in his chest. She felt his body vibrate with laughter as his arms came around her and snugged her close. She had a single heartbeat to contemplate how well they fit together despite the difference in size, and then she felt the indescribable sensation of her body dissolving as the world spun away.

Certain Dimitri would keep her safe, her curiosity overcame her apprehension and Elle drew a deep breath and cracked one eye open. Then both eyes opened wide. Or at least she thought they did. Although she could still feel Dimitri solid and warm along the length of her body, neither of them appeared to have any substance. Racing ribbons of color and light surrounded them, weaving complicated patterns in the air as the city streaked by below. She was weightless, flying, nothing but molecules absorbed by the wind, yet oddly separate. Her heart hammered against her ribs at an alarming speed and she wondered how it continued to beat when she no longer had a body. The sensation was terrifying, impossible, exhilarating. She felt, rather than saw, Dimitri smile as she opened her heart and mind to embrace the experience, knowing even though she'd made a career of manipulating words, she would never be able to describe this to anyone, ever. She simply had nothing with which to compare it.

"Hang on." Dimitri's voice echoed in the air and her knees buckled at the suddenness of her body's reformation. She would have collapsed into a puddle at her angel's feet if his arms hadn't continued to support her as her feet found purchase on solid ground once again. As the room spun, Elle closed her eyes and forcibly swallowed down the bile rising to scald the back of her throat when an unexpected wave of nausea struck. Dimitri continued to hold her patiently, his big hands gently stroking up and down the length of her back while she struggled to regain her equilibrium.

"Just breathe, baby. Remember what I told you earlier? In through your nose and out through your mouth... smell a rose, blow out a candle. Okay?"

Elle nodded her forehead against his chest and relaxed the death grip she had around his solid middle.

"That was...uh, wow! But maybe next time we should just take a cab?" Elle laughed unsteadily.

"You'll get used to it," Dimitri predicted before dropping a kiss on the top of her head, scooping her up, and depositing her on an enormous leather sofa in front of a massive stone fireplace. He plucked a green chenille throw from the back of a nearby chair and tucked it snugly around her before stepping over to the wall and flicking a switch that set the gas logs blazing to life. The fire cast a warm orange glow that pierced the darkness and gave Elle her first glimpse of the place Dimitri Radchenko called home.

"Get used to it? Doubtful," Elle mumbled skeptically.

"Will coffee help?" Dimitri strode back to the sofa and dropped Elle's bag on the floor at the far end.

"Never hurts." She squinted through the dimness hoping for some insight about this man for whom she felt so much, yet knew so little. To her left, a wall comprised entirely of windows opened onto an enormous terrace. Such expansive outdoor space was an incredible luxury in the city. Beyond the patio, the city reflected in a breathtaking view on the waters of the Hudson, while across the river, New Jersey twinkled like a box of confused Christmas lights trailing off into the distance. Given the perspective, Elle guesstimated they were somewhere south of Canal Street. To her right, a wall covered from floor to fifteen foot ceiling in bookshelves extended all the way back to the breakfast bar beyond which Dimitri puttered about in the small but fully equipped kitchen. Dark, gleaming hardwood floors scattered with colorful area rugs ran the length of the space and continued on into a hallway next to the kitchen, which Elle assumed led to the bedrooms. The space felt open and airy, yet cozy and intimate. A place of impossible contradiction, just like Dimitri.

Elle tossed the throw aside and wandered over to the bookshelves marveling at the incredible variety. Thick, tattered volumes of indeterminate age vied for space with medical reference books and the glossy jackets of current best sellers. Elle grinned as she noticed a few of her own romances among the collection. She glanced in Dimitri's direction, but refrained from commenting. She closed her eyes, drew in a long, deep breath through her nose, and momentarily held it as a faint, satisfied smile curled her lips.

"What are you doing?" Dimitri asked.

"Smelling the magic," Elle mumbled as heat rushed into her face.

"Excuse me?" Dimitri stopped in the middle of pouring the coffee to regard her with a curious expression.

"Growing up in such isolation, books were all I knew. They were magic to me. I could travel to distant places, meet fascinating people, lose myself in someone else's reality, you know? When I was younger, I believed if I concentrated hard enough when surrounded by books, I could smell the magic." She shrugged self-consciously. "Silly, huh?"

"No, I don't think it's silly at all," he responded quietly. "Lonely people invent ways to endure."

Something in the tone of his voice told her he was speaking from experience.

"So what did you invent? To endure."

Dimitri's massive shoulders rose and fell. "I paint a little."

The aroma of Columbian dark roast tickled her

nostrils as Elle wandered back to the sofa and tucked her legs beneath her to make room for Dimitri as his footsteps approached. He squeezed in next to her after handing her a steaming mug and taking a tentative sip from his own.

"Feel better?"

"Yeah, thanks. I guess coffee can cure just about everything." Elle sighed into her cup.

"Well, the physician in me takes issue with that, but if it works for you, I won't argue," Dimitri laughed.

"So how long have you been a doctor?"

"Graduated med school in nineteen fifty-seven. Practiced until the early eighties."

"Why did you stop?"

"I got tired of watching people die. Too often I had the power to save them but couldn't do so without opening up a huge can of worms."

"Because it would have required methods you couldn't explain?"

"Exactly."

"That must have been difficult."

"Sweetness, you have no idea."

"I'm sorry."

"Don't be. Not your fault. And realistically it wasn't like I could have saved them all. Even *Earthbound* have limits. But the ones I could have saved? Yeah, they haunt me."

"Well, it might not be my fault, but it wasn't yours either and I'm sorry for bringing it up. Clearly, it's painful for you. It's just…well, I feel like I know so little about you when it comes down to it."

"Guess I do know a helluva lot more about you than you do about me. What do you want to know?"

Dimitri set his cup on the end table and turned slightly so they were half sitting, half lying on the sofa with Elle reclining against his chest. It didn't escape her notice that in this position she was unable to read his expression. She suspected it was deliberate.

"Really?"

"Really."

"Okay. Let's see…after you saved me from the rabid squirrel, you said you grew up on a farm. Where was it?"

"A little village in the Caucasus region, near the Caspian Sea. And the squirrel wasn't rabid. He was twice as scared as you were."

Elle handed her cup over her head to Dimitri and snuggled into him even more deeply when she heard the clunk indicating he'd deposited it on the table near his own.

"Says you. He looked crazed and vicious to me. So how did you go from farm boy to *Defensori*? Manhattan is a long way away from a village in the Caucasus."

"Thousands of miles and hundreds of lifetimes away," Dimitri agreed quietly. Elle felt him tense beneath her and she turned so she was lying along his side, her arm draped across his flat stomach, her cheek against his chest. She listened to the steady, dependable beat of his heart for several minutes, waiting for him to continue. He scrubbed a hand over his face and remained silent.

"Dimitri," Elle raised her head and propped her chin on his chest to look him full in the face. "You're safe with me, you know. Your secrets, your heart…they're safe with me. Because *you've* given *me* that. Safety. You didn't judge me, didn't turn away when you learned the truth. For the first time in my entire life, here with you, I feel completely safe. Like no one can ever threaten me again. I never dreamed I could have that kind of security. So, yeah, I want to know everything there is to know about you. But if you aren't ready to talk about this, it's okay. I'm not going anywhere."

Dimitri's eyes warmed with an emotion Elle couldn't quite identify. He reached to cup her face in his big hand, stroking his thumb along her cheekbone, before picking up his head to brush his lips lightly along hers. Then he pushed her head back against his chest and drew in a deep breath expelling it with a sigh.

"I just…I guess I don't want you to think less of me when you realize I'm the kind of guy who holds a grudge. Pretty much forever."

"You forget I'm holding a couple of grudges of my own." Elle burrowed her fingers beneath the hem of his tee to stroke the silky skin beneath.

"I doubt you're capable of the same degree of venom, but point taken."

"So your family had a farm in a village near the Caspian Sea," Elle prompted deciding subtlety was overrated.

"Yeah. We were one of several *Earthbound* families in the area. All *Earthbound* aren't warriors. Some simply live among the general population and work to thwart the evil influence of the *Fallen* by example. It was around the time Genghis Khan was slaughtering his way through Eurasia and building his empire."

"Genghis Khan? You knew Genghis Khan?" Elle

squeaked, attempting to pick up her head. Dimitri's hand held her firmly in place. She knew he was hundreds of years old, of course, but she hadn't considered exactly what that entailed before now. Truthfully, it freaked her out just a little, especially when she reflected on the very real possibility she faced the same fate. On the other hand, the life experience alone could provide the fodder for a great book. If she ever decided to resume her career when this whole mess was over, she might seriously think about exploring other genres. Against all odds, her exposé on Jack the Ripper had done remarkably well. It was certainly something to consider.

"No, I didn't know Genghis Khan," he shot back in an exasperated tone. "Now do you want to hear this or don't you?"

"Sorry." Elle snuggled back into his side. Any story starting with Genghis Khan as a lead in could not end well. This was a man who'd sat quietly in her darkened bedroom night after night for weeks just so she wouldn't be frightened and alone when she woke from the nightmare. Now she was asking him to revisit a period in his life she suspected was going to be painful, whether centuries had passed or not. As much as she'd wanted to know, she was increasingly sorry she'd asked.

"We'd heard the stories, of course, but weren't particularly worried in our isolated little corner of the world. After all, what could we possibly have that anyone would want? Some grain? Couple of cows? We'd heard the Khan was heading back to the Mongolian steppes after defeating the Khwarezmian Empire. But we didn't know he'd split his forces and sent twenty thousand men into the Caucasus on a mission led by one of his most trusted generals, a man named Jebe. Jebe's troops encircled the entire Caspian Sea, destroying everyone and everything in their path."

"Including your family?" Elle whispered into his chest.

Dimitri grunted his assent.

"But you survived."

"Yeah. I survived. I'd sneaked off trying to avoid chores. I guess I didn't take duty or responsibility quite so seriously in those days. I found myself a nice big tree a couple hundred feet into the woods and was just getting comfortable when the ground started to shake. I didn't know what the hell it was so I just held on for dear life and waited. The Mongol's troops passed right underneath me and never knew I was there. By the time I climbed down and ran back to our cottage, it was too late."

"You can't blame yourself, Dimitri. You couldn't know what was coming and you couldn't have prevented it. You were just a little boy doing what little boys do."

"Our cottage was burning, my mother screaming inside," he continued as though she hadn't spoken. "That bastard sat there on his big white horse with his troops around him and watched it burn. Watched everything burn. I didn't stop to think. I just turned and ran right through the front door with his laughter ringing in my ears. I guess he figured I was a goner anyway so he didn't bother trying to stop me. I could hardly see through the smoke and breathing was damn near impossible. I crawled along the floor feeling my way until I found my mother. She was already dead. I tried to drag her out, but I was too young, too weak. I tripped over something and when I fell, she landed on top of me. Her body protected mine when the house collapsed."

"Oh my God." Elle's breath caught on a sob. "Why? What did he have to gain by attacking a village full of helpless farmers?"

"Jebe, the Khan's general, was a *Fallen*. I felt him as soon as I got close enough. Reconnaissance was probably the excuse he sold the Khan, but annihilation of *Earthbound* was his real motive. His troops were armed with Hell forged weapons though I doubt most of them knew the difference. I may have been too weak to stop him then, but I'm not weak anymore. If the bastard still walks this earth, I'll find him eventually."

"You became a *Defensori* to avenge your family," Elle whispered.

"I became a *Defensori* to avenge *every* family the *Fallen* has destroyed, whether human or *Earthbound*."

She noticed he never mentioned that when not killing the evil ones, he'd devoted his life to the sick, the wounded, and the weak. Like her. She suspected it was as much a penance as a calling. Elle propped her chin on his chest and looked at Dimitri through a thick veil of tears and saw him. Really saw him. The scars on his face were nothing compared to those he carried inside. Behind the bone melting sex appeal, under the massive, threatening, leather clad exterior, buried beneath the hard ass bad boy facade, lived a guilt-ridden little boy who believed he'd failed his family and had been trying to atone for it ever since.

"Don't look at me like that," he growled in a low, rough tone she'd never heard him use. Shifting free of her body, he jumped to his feet and stalked to the windows where he crossed his arms over his chest and stared into the darkness with his back to her. "There're a lot of things I want from you, Elle. Pity isn't one of them."

"Well, fortunately, I wasn't offering any." Elle cleared her throat and climbed slowly to her feet. Dimitri remained an immobile statue silhouetted against the window as she approached from behind and tentatively slid her arms around his waist, splaying her hands across the hard muscles of his abdomen and resting her cheek against his back.

"Weren't you?" He asked quietly. "I think maybe you were. God knows I've seen the look in my line of work more times than I can remember. Hell, I'm pretty sure I've *worn* it more times than I can remember. I'm usually pretty good at picking up on it."

Elle drew in a deep breath and let it out slowly. Then she pressed her lips to the back of his shoulder before continuing.

"Okay, maybe there was a *little* pity involved. I'm sorry if that offends you, but I won't apologize for it. I can't ignore my heart to protect your pride. Anyway, the pity wasn't for the man you are today, you don't need it. It was for that little boy who lost everything and everyone and was left all alone to find his way in the world."

"Yeah, well…" His shoulders lifted and fell. "He did okay. Buried the dead, scavenged what he could, and eventually found a human couple who gave him a home and the semblance of a family in exchange for his labor."

"Buried the dead?" Elle whispered. "You buried

them...your parents, your neighbors, all of them?"

"There was no one else left to do it," he said in a matter-of-fact tone revealing nothing of the horror he must have endured and Elle's heart shattered into pieces all over again. It didn't escape her that Dimitri spoke of the child he'd been in the third person, as though the child was someone else entirely. Clearly, he'd had to find a way to compartmentalize that period of his life, to keep the boy at a distance in order to survive.

"There were some I never found, of course. Maybe they escaped, maybe they burned to ash." He shrugged his massive shoulders as though acknowledging it was a puzzle he would never solve. "You hungry?"

Chapter Fifteen

"What?"

With an effort, Elle shook her head to clear her mind of the horrific visuals his story evoked and forced her thoughts back into the here and now. Obviously, Dimitri had revisited enough of his past for one night and was ready to change the subject. He turned in her arms and pulled her against him, resting his chin on the top of her head.

"I mean no, I'm not hungry."

"Well, I am." He cupped her buttocks through her jeans and ground his hips against her, making it clear without words the hunger he referred to wasn't going to be sated by a couple of burgers and a chocolate shake. "I think I need to indulge in something very life affirming about now."

Elle tipped her head back and saw the heat in his dark gaze. Her pulse thrummed in response to the promise she saw lurking there. Breath rushed painfully into her lungs as a low, simmering heat curled in her stomach and spread outward causing a heavy ache in her breasts. As it moved lower, she pressed her thighs together and fought the urge to squirm. She imagined brushing her lips along the broad, smooth expanse of his chest, pressing them to that delicious spot where his long neck joined his shoulder. She swallowed hard and a shiver rolled over her skin. He flashed a devilish smile that told her he was fully aware of her reaction and was enjoying it immensely. When he finally lowered his head to capture her mouth, Elle leaned into him with a sigh. One big hand slid under her sweater to cup an aching breast through the lace of her bra while the other snaked below the waistband of her jeans to cup her bare buttocks and pull her more intimately against him. He rocked his hips and desire consumed her right down to her fingertips as the hard evidence of his arousal ground insistently against the juncture of her thighs.

His mouth slanted over hers again and again, his tongue probing, stroking, and tangling frantically with hers, as they stumbled across the room in a shameless dance. By the time the smooth fabric of the sofa caressed the backs of her legs, she realized her jeans were missing, her clothing was strewn across the floor, and they were both already too far gone to make it to his bed. His hands were everywhere at once and Elle went up in flames as she tugged at the zipper of his jeans to free his straining erection. When at last her fingers closed around the hard, pulsing length of him, his groan seemed to come from somewhere deep in his soul. She collapsed back onto the sofa, and he kicked off his jeans before coming down on top of her, supporting his weight on his forearms, and positioning himself between her thighs.

"So damn soft," he mumbled against her breast. He rolled a hard nipple between his lips and bit down gently. Then he eased the sting with his tongue before focusing his attention on her other breast. His clever fingers caressed her from waist to her hip, back and forth, over and over, until at last his hand slipped between their bodies and began stroking her to the verge of madness. She couldn't think, couldn't speak, couldn't feel anything but Dimitri and the delicious sensations gathering with painful sweetness at her core. She arched against him seeking release but suddenly he propped himself up on one elbow and stilled, gazing down at her intently.

"Are you sure, baby?" he whispered tightly. Beads of perspiration dotted his forehead as he struggled to hold himself back.

She picked up her head and her eyes widened in disbelief.

"*Now*? You're asking me that *now*? You've got to be kidding!"

"I just …there's something you should know first."

"Can you please give me the condensed version?" she panted impatiently.

"This thing between us…that is, I don't know how much Gatewick or Kat told you, but it's different for *Earthbound*. If we make love and you're my bound mate, my other half, as I suspect you are, you'll pretty much be stuck with me. We'll be tied together for a long, long time. I just don't want you to have any regrets."

Elle took his face in her hands and stared directly into those dark, loving eyes. She'd never seen Dimitri anything but completely confident and the uncertainty she saw lurking in their brown depths touched her heart in a way nothing else could. Though surrounded by people, he'd been alone for so long, yet he'd still been willing to sacrifice his happiness for hers. Any doubts, any hesitation, any question of whether binding herself to this man was the right thing to do evaporated into the mist, put to rest by the depth of emotion reflected in her warrior's eyes.

"Dimitri Radchenko, you big lug, I love you. Yes, I do," she nodded emphatically when his eyes widened. "I mean, I know it all seems to have happened very quickly and you don't have to say it back or anything, but the only thing I'm going to regret at this point is if you can't finish what you started."

"Is that a challenge?" He arched a brow and grinned, leaning forward to feather his lips along the line of her jaw before capturing her lips in a tender kiss. Then he buried his face in her neck as though it hurt to look at her and took a deep, shuddering breath.

"Afraid you're not up for it?" She reached between them and curled her fingers around his rigid flesh, her lips twitching into a smug grin when his breath hitched and he shifted uncomfortably.

"Oh, I think I'm up for it," he growled and resumed his attentive stroking of her sensitive, moisture slicked nub with renewed enthusiasm. "I just hope you are. And Elle? Baby, I love you, too."

The declaration alone nearly put her over the edge. With a groan, Elle closed her eyes and gave herself up to the exquisite sensations reverberating through her body as her thighs quivered and her stomach muscles tightened in anticipation of the coming storm.

"Dimitri?" she panted breathlessly. "In me. Now."

She didn't have to ask twice. Elle moaned as she arched toward him and he filled the emptiness within her. An emptiness that transcended the physical. A gaping hole in the very fabric of her being she hadn't even known was there. He grasped her hips and as soon as her muscles began to relax and accommodate his size, he hammered hard and deep, quickening his pace as her thighs quaked and her body tightened around him. She bit into her lower lip and dug her fingers into his shoulders as she locked her ankles behind his back to draw him even closer. They were both covered with a fine sheen of sweat and Dimitri's eyes were glued to her face as though he was reading every expression, every nuance. Clenching his jaw, he adjusted his angle, thrusting deeper and faster.

"Come with me, baby," he growled roughly. "Come. With. Me. Now."

His fingers dug into her hips and she rose to meet every thrust as he slammed into her over and over, erupting inside her as she tightened and pulsed around him, crossing a pleasure threshold she'd never even come close to and couldn't ever have imagined existed. She floated somewhere beyond rational thought, losing herself, anchored only by the intense pleasure of Dimitri's hard body moving inside her. Shields down, mind completely open, she allowed Dimitri to experience everything she was feeling, stunned to realize that in that moment, she could sense him as well. It was a moment of incredible completeness and as she drifted slowly back to Earth, she had the odd but unmistakable sensation of invisible threads wrapping around them and binding them together heart, mind, and soul.

"Shit! That was…wow. Just wow," he groaned against her neck as he finally stilled. A shudder went through him and he picked his head up to look at her, his dark hair forming a curtain around his face, the ends brushing against her shoulders. His eyes burned with some intense emotion she'd never seen there before.

Stroking her damp hair away from her forehead, he lowered his head and pressed his lips there. Her eyes filled reflexively at the unconsciously tender gesture.

"Hey, you okay?" he asked gently, his brows slamming together. "I planned to go slow the first time, but the feel of you… damn, I just… lost it. I didn't hurt you, did I?"

"You planned? So you've been giving this a little thought, eh, Big Guy?" Elle laughed softly, tucking a damp strand of dark hair behind his ear. "For how long exactly?"

"A while," he muttered evasively. "Can't you ever just answer a damn question?"

"No, you didn't hurt me, okay? In fact, if I felt any better I might just dissolve into a puddle." Stretching up, she pressed her lips to his, loving the salty taste of him, and bit back a smile at his relieved expression. "There at the end, did you feel that?"

"Sweetness, I'd have had to be dead not to."

"Not *that*, you idiot," she slapped playfully at his shoulder.

"The binding? Yeah, I felt it."

"So that means we're…?"

"It means we're bound mates. It means you're stuck with me for the rest of our natural lives, however long they may be. It means our souls are two halves of a whole that have finally found their way home and even if you leave me tomorrow, no one will ever complete you the way I do. In short, it means you're *mine*. I did give you a chance to change your mind." Dimitri grinned, looking happier and more relaxed than Elle had ever seen him.

"Never let it be said I don't like to live

dangerously." Elle grinned back as she twined her fingers in his hair and tugged his head down. But as his lips touched hers, her smile faded and she pulled back as a thought occurred to her. What if she didn't have *Earthbound* longevity and was destined to live a brief, mortal life? Not that she'd ever had any other expectations before tonight, but what about Dimitri? He as much as said he'd fought the bond between them when he believed she was human and would die. Had he only given in to his feelings completely once they suspected she might be around longer than anyone originally thought? And if that was the case, what if they were wrong?

"Listen to me," Elle tugged at his hair until he raised his head. "I need you to promise me something."

"Yeah, we'll make it last all night next time if you want."

"Not that," she thumped his chest impatiently, smiling despite herself at his cheeky response. "I'm serious."

"Okay, shoot." He let out a long, pained sigh and shifted to his back, rolling her over on top of him and pulling the throw from the back of the sofa to settle it over both of them.

"It's just…well, if we're wrong, if I have nothing more than a few good decades in me, I want you to promise me you'll be okay. We have no way of knowing if I'll have longevity like the rest of you and I don't want my death to be one more sorrow you carry around after I'm gone. Gah, I just realized how arrogant that must sound. I mean it's not like you haven't suffered losses that makes losing me look like peanuts. It's just when you thought I was completely human…"

"Now *you* listen." Dimitri buried his hands in her hair, cupping her face in his hands, and staring directly into her eyes. "Whether I lose you tomorrow or a century from now, it'll never hurt less. And don't ever think losing you would amount to nothing more than…what did you call it? Peanuts?" His lips twisted in a faint grin. "Apparently you still don't fully understand what I feel for you, woman. The bottom line is, either of us could die tomorrow or both of us could live for centuries. Nothing is guaranteed. It took me a long time to realize that and understand nothing I do can change it. What matters is now, so how about we let tomorrow worry about itself?"

"You think you can do that?"

"I can try. Turns out avoiding attachments really is a pretty effective mechanism for avoiding grief. You can't lose what you don't care about, right? But it's a half-life. It's empty. I don't want to be empty anymore. I want this. I want you. For however long I can have you. Say it again."

"I love you," she breathed into his mouth as his lips captured hers in a tender kiss. When he drew away at last, he shifted his body, exposing the text inked on his ribcage. Elle ran a fingertip gently along the lines.

"Is this French? What does this say?"

"*He who has gone, so we but cherish his memory, abides with us, more potent, nay, more present than the living man.* It's a quote from Antoine de Saint-Exupéry, a French aristocrat and writer. Basically, it means we never truly lose people as long as they live on in our hearts. I believed that once but I guess I let myself forget for a while."

"Well, I don't plan on becoming a memory

anytime soon, but just in case, maybe I should work on giving you something to remember." Elle narrowed her eyes.

"Ah, sweetness, you already have, you have no idea how much. But, hey, if you feel the need to put a little more effort into it, you won't get any arguments from me," he growled, tugging her hair to bring her lips down to his.

Elle lost herself in the rough touch of his hands, the feel of sleek muscle rippling beneath warm satin where her hands rested on his chest, the light scrape of his beard against her throat as he nuzzled there. Her heart raced at the way he breathed her name into her mouth before recapturing her lips.

"The bed would be a lot more comfortable," he murmured against her mouth.

"M'kay," she nipped at his lower lip with her teeth before pushing up from his chest. "Let's..." Elle froze halfway to her feet and grabbed for the throw, wrapping it around herself with a shriek. "There's someone out there!"

"Where?" Dimitri came to his feet in one fluid movement, pushing her behind him at the same time.

"The terrace," she gasped in a shaky voice. "There's someone out there watching us." Gripping his shoulder, she felt the tension in him, but as she leaned to peek around him, his muscles eased under her hand.

"Galen," he announced with a grunt. "Relax, the windows are tinted. He can't see a thing."

Dimitri bent and gathered up her clothes, pressing them into her arms and jerking his chin in the direction of the hallway. "Go ahead and get dressed."

Snagging his pants from the floor, he poked his

legs into them and yanked them up over his hips before moving toward the sliding doors. Elle clutched her things against her chest with one hand while holding the throw around her with the other and hurried in the direction he'd indicated.

Dimitri stepped to the glass, cranked the latch to the left, and slid open the door, moving aside as Galen stepped in dragging two suitcases behind him.

"Thanks, brother. I appreciate this. I know Elle will, too." Dimitri grabbed the luggage Elle abandoned at the hotel that morning and placed it to the side, waving Galen to a chair and heading toward the kitchen. "Beer?"

"Sure. Found them in the manager's office. Don't think anyone had time yet to help themselves to anything." Galen unzipped his leather jacket and dropped his ass into the chair. Stretching his long legs out in front of him, he crossed one booted foot over the other and reached for the beer Dimitri offered, taking a long pull. "Thanks."

"It's probably just clothes. She's too smart to have left anything of value behind. They give you any trouble about claiming them?"

"Hard to say since I didn't exactly ask," Galen chuckled and Dimitri joined in as he dropped onto the sofa.

"So what'd you find out?"

"You just assume it's been such a quiet night I went and checked out Gatewick's compound?" Galen arched a brow in Dimitri's direction.

"Well, let's see… you're here on a luggage delivery mission, parked on your ass, and drinking a beer so, yeah, I figured maybe you had some time on your hands."

"Point taken." Galen tipped the bottle in Dimitri's direction with a grin before tilting it to his lips again. "Well, the place was right where Elle said it was. According to the sign, it's an embryonic cryogenic storage facility."

"Well, isn't that convenient?" Dimitri's lip curled.

"Well, it sure as hell gives him easy access doesn't it? If he's the one keeping the records, who's going to notice if he helps himself to a frozen embryo or two for his own personal use? On the surface, the place looks like any other commercial building. But, something doesn't add up. I couldn't sense any mental activity, even though I saw at least two men enter the building while I watched. It was like the door closed behind them and they dropped off the grid."

"The lab and living quarters are constructed below ground," Elle announced woodenly as she shuffled back into the room in bare feet, her face flushed. Dimitri shifted on the sofa to make a space for her but she veered away and chose the chair next to the sofa and across from Galen instead. "From the inside, you can't tell the living space is anything other than a real house. Very cozy, actually, but in reality it's more like a secured bunker. I guess I should have thought the whole set-up was odd, but for years I never had any notion my home was any different from anyone else's and when I did figure it out, Gatewick explained it away as a necessary evil required for security purposes."

"You think that area is blocked somehow?"

Elle shrugged as though it made no difference to her one way or another.

"What's wrong with you?"

Elle jumped and turned wide eyes in his direction as the thought he sent registered in her mind. He'd known as bound mates they would be able to communicate telepathically but he'd simply forgotten to mention it to Elle. He figured she'd have to forgive his oversight since it was her fault he'd been so pleasantly distracted in the first place. Just thinking of how pleasantly distracted got him hard as steel all over again. Instead of answering, she simply pressed her lips together and shook her head slightly before turning her attention back to Galen. Dimitri frowned. While there might be a lot of things he'd yet to learn about his mate, he knew her well enough to know when she was avoiding a question.

"Galen didn't see a thing, if that's what has you worried."

"Are those my suitcases?" Elle jumped up suddenly and moved toward the luggage still sitting by the windows.

"Yeah, I asked Galen to get them from the hotel." Dimitri frowned harder, pushing up from the sofa to his feet. What exactly crawled up her ass in the last five minutes? "It's too risky for either of us to be seen at your place at the moment and I thought you might like to have some of your own things."

"Thank you, Galen. That was very nice of you." She threw the words over her shoulder without turning around, thus missing Galen's casual shrug, and ignoring Dimitri completely. "In fact, since I have something to change into now, I think I'd like to take a shower if you don't mind."

"Why would I mind?"

Elle shrugged, bent to unzip the larger of the

suitcases, and dug through the contents, tugging out a pair of faded jeans and an oversized sweatshirt. Tossing them on the floor beside her, she dug into an inside pocket for undies, then gathered everything together and rose to her feet. Dimitri came up right behind her, blocking her path, but she simply stepped around him as though he were a piece of inconveniently placed furniture.

"Thanks again, Galen. Now if you'll excuse me?" Without so much as a glance in Dimitri's direction, she spun on her heel and hurried down the hall toward the bathroom with the urgency of someone being pursued by demons.

What the hell?

Chapter Sixteen

Elle barely registered the low buzz of conversation behind her as Galen prepared to take his leave. She rushed into the bathroom, closed and locked the door, and leaned against it, allowing her clothes to slip from her trembling fingers to the floor. Dimitri's bathroom was surprisingly large for a city apartment, sleek and modern, chrome and granite, but Elle was far too distracted to appreciate the designer elegance or the alluring scent of leather, soap, and Dimitri permeating the space. When Galen appeared and she'd hightailed down the hall to dress, she'd initially stumbled into the second bedroom that Dimitri apparently used as a studio. When he'd said he painted a little as a way to endure loneliness, he may have been just a bit too modest. He was good, beyond good, really. It wasn't so much that she'd been surprised to discover his incredible talent. It wasn't that she was dumbfounded by his ability to flawlessly capture life-like realism. No, it was the subject of the portrait leaning against the studio wall which caused her pulse to race and her heart to doubt everything they'd just shared. No wonder Dimitri had found her past so easy to swallow. He'd probably known the truth all along.

Elle held her breath and swallowed hard over the painful lump in her throat as Dimitri's measured tread approached the door. She simply could not comprehend misjudging him so completely. He couldn't have simulated the actual binding. She'd felt the sensation and knew it was real. But just because they were meant for one another in some convoluted cosmic destiny didn't mean he actually had to *feel* anything for her. *That* could be faked. Had she really let her desire for love and acceptance—and okay, her desire for Dimitri—blindly lead her down a fools' path to a land of lies only to discover she was a means to an end, yet again? God, would she never learn?

Elle gasped and awkwardly knuckled the moisture from her eyes as the doorknob rattled. Whatever happened, she would never give him the satisfaction of knowing how deeply his subterfuge had wounded her.

"Elle, open the door."

"I'm getting in the shower," she croaked in a voice, that even to her own ears, sounded thick with tears.

"The shower isn't going anywhere. Now open the door and talk to me."

"Why don't you just go out with Galen and kill something? I really don't want to talk to you right now."

Elle heard him draw in and blow out a deep breath and then suddenly he was in the bathroom, standing right in front of her.

"Hey, that's not fair!"

"I never claimed to be fair. Now what's your problem?"

Elle bit her lip and risked a glance at his face. His brows were drawn together, pleating his forehead and somehow combining impatience, exasperation, and tenderness all in one expression. Her stomach somersaulted at the genuine concern she saw in his eyes, and then she hardened her heart and straightened her spine. What *was* her problem? She was smart and resourceful and wrote stories about strong, independent heroines who didn't wait for the hero to come along and make life worth living. Well, she could be that way too, right? So maybe she'd fallen hard for a big, ass-kicking angel with a soft spot he kept carefully hidden, but apparently, she'd given him too much credit. Even angels could have a secret agenda. It wasn't like betrayal was a new experience. She could suck this up just like she's sucked up everything else in her life. She would survive. She always had.

"Fine, you want to know what my problem is? I saw the painting." Pouting and biting her tongue wouldn't solve a thing. He wanted to know, then fine. She would call him on it and let him explain it. If he could.

His brows lowered even further. "So, let me get this straight. You're pissed I have a hobby?"

"Don't be deliberately obtuse, Radchenko. No wonder you came back night after night. Guardian Angel, my ass. It was never about me, never about my nightmares, was it? It was always about you and gaining revenge for what you'd lost. Did it ever enter that big, thick skull of yours that you could have simply asked me? It would have been a lot kinder than leading me to believe you actually cared."

"I'm pretty sure I'll be deeply insulted and completely pissed once I figure out what you're talking about."

"The painting you dim-wit! Did you honestly think I'd never find out? "

Dimitri's brows flew in the opposite direction as

though a light bulb had suddenly come on over his head and the tension in his posture visibly eased.

"Oh, that! Well damn, it wasn't some deep, dark secret, but I could hardly carry it around in my wallet to show you, either." The man grinned audaciously, but it quickly faded to a look of uncertainty as she continued to glower at him. "Frankly, I didn't expect you to get upset being my subject. I take it you don't like it? Maybe I should paint you wearing my T-shirt?"

"What in the hell are you talking about?" Elle ground out through teeth clenched so tightly her jaw was beginning to ache.

Dimitri dropped his chin to his chest and pinched the bridge of his nose between a thumb and forefinger. "Okay, let's try this again. What in the hell are *you* talking about?"

"*Chen*! The big honking portrait of Chen in your studio!"

"What?"

A deep growl clawed its way out of Elle's chest as she spun and wrenched the door open. Then she stomped across the hallway into the studio as Dimitri followed slowly behind. Her stomach churned like an industrial mixer and she swallowed back the bile, praying she wouldn't embarrass herself by actually being sick. She couldn't be mistaken about the face in the portrait, a face she knew as well as her own. She couldn't believe he was going to play dumb and expect her to buy it. But dear God, she wanted to. If everything they'd shared was nothing but a ploy, she knew it would destroy something inside her she might never recover.

"Well?" She demanded as she halted in front of the

canvas, annoyed to realize her voice was shaky and not nearly as firm and defiant as she'd intended.

"Well what?" Dimitri roared, throwing his hands in the air. "If you have something to say, just spit it out. Never was much good at games."

"This...this," she gestured at the portrait of an Asian man in a red silk tunic covered by an armor vest constructed of small rectangular bronze plates laced together in horizontal rows. "He's Jebe, the *Fallen* you've been hunting for hundreds of years isn't he? I guess you'd like me to believe it's a coincidence that these days he's known as Justin Chen, the man behind the money behind John Gatewick. You knew! You knew the truth about me all the time, didn't you? I'm nothing more to you than a way to get to him!"

Dimitri froze and the eyes looking out at her were suddenly the cold, dead stare of a venomous snake.

"You know this man?" He barely whispered the words, but the tone was lethal.

"Don't pretend that comes as a surprise. All those nights, sitting in the dark, seeing my nightmares, examining my memories. I thought..." Elle's voice cracked. "I *hoped* you kept coming back because you were beginning to care about *me,* when all the time you were just looking for a way to get to *him.*"

For long, painful heartbeats, he continued to regard her with that hard angry stare. Then something flared in the depths of his dark eyes.

"If you regret what just happened, Arabella, say so. You don't have to fabricate excuses to push me away. I'm going out for a while. Do *not* leave this apartment," Dimitri growled before turning to leave.

"That's it?" Elle cried in devastated disbelief. "You

aren't even going to deny it?"

"No."

"I…see." Feeling as though someone had just kicked her in the stomach, Elle resisted the urge to wrap her arms around herself and double over from the pain. She'd offered him everything, and he was walking out the door. She refused to let him see how deeply she was hurting. If pride was all she had left to call her own, then by damn she'd hang onto it with ragged, bloody fingernails.

"Actually it's pretty clear you don't see at all. I'll be back in a couple of hours. Do *not* leave this apartment."

"What do you care?" Elle tossed her head defiantly. "You got what you wanted. There really isn't any point in me sticking around, is there?"

"Baby, I'm a patient man, but you're really pushing right now. I'll be back in a couple of hours, by which time I may have cooled down enough to talk to you about this. But right at this moment? Not so much. Go take a shower and go to bed. Or don't. Just stay inside." Without another word or glance, he stalked from the room and seconds later the front door slammed with enough force to rattle the walls.

Once he was gone, Elle gave up all pretense of control and allowed her trembling legs to buckle beneath her. Alone on the cold, hard floor of the empty studio, she hugged her knees to her chest. Dropping her forehead onto them, she let the tears come. She was dumbfounded at his departure. Wondering how she could have misjudged him so completely, she was unable to believe she'd trusted in someone's love only to discover she'd been nothing but a pawn in a game she'd never agreed to play. Again. As the tears soaked through the knees of her jeans, she gasped for breath over the thick plug of grief clogging her throat and desperately wished for the familiarity of Kat's apartment where she could wrap herself in her mind-numbing misery, sensing somehow Kat would know how to make her feel better. She'd no sooner pictured the place in her mind when with a whoosh of air and a dizzying ribbon of light, she found herself sitting on the floor of the McAllister's living room. She picked her head up and looked around slowly, stunned to realize she'd somehow managed to fade without knowing how or having the slightest inkling she was able to do so. *How the hell had that happened?*

"Oh my God, my eyes!" Elle screeched as Kassian McAllister strolled casually out of the kitchen with a bottle of beer in one hand and a bottle of water in the other, wearing nothing but a smile that quickly morphed into a shocked scowl.

"Where in the hell did you come from?" Deftly transferring both bottles to one hand, he snatched the chenille throw from the back of the sofa and held it strategically in front of himself.

"I have no idea," Elle groaned from behind the fingers she'd slapped over her eyes. "All I wanted was to see a friendly face, and now I'm going to pay for it by going blind."

"Stifle your inner drama queen, woman. It's not like you haven't seen a naked man before."

"Not without prior notice and definitely not my best friend's husband." Elle peeked from between her fingers and seeing he'd managed to sufficiently cover himself, dropped her hands and climbed to her feet.

"Although at the risk of sounding completely inappropriate, I'm beginning to understand what Kat sees in you."

"Completely inappropriate. Thanks, I think," McAllister set the bottles on a nearby table and securely fastened the throw around his waist like a sarong. "Now what are you doing here, how did you get in, and where's Dimitri?"

Before Elle could open her mouth to formulate an answer, Kat came striding from the bedroom, tightening the belt of a blue, silk robe and tossing a black one to her husband.

"Stop badgering her, Kassian. Can't you see she's upset?"

"But how did she just pop in here?" McAllister muttered, turning his back and slipping on the robe, then he bent to scoop up the throw and toss it on a nearby chair.

"Didn't you drop the *sigils* to let Dimitri and Elle fade out from here?" Kat arched a brow in her husband's direction.

"Well, yeah…"

"And did you remember to put them back up after they left?"

"Uh…shit! Distracted. Your fault." McAllister stepped toward the door with a dark frown and began to move his hands in an intricate pattern in the air, resetting the protective *sigils* around the entrance to the penthouse.

Kat grabbed Elle's hand and pulled her down on the couch beside her.

"Now what's wrong? And how *did* you get here? Where's Dimitri?"

"Dimitri's gone. I don't know where he is, and furthermore, I don't care. As to how I got here, I was wallowing, you know how well I can do that when I set my mind to it, and wishing I was here with you to hash it all out, and suddenly I was." Elle shrugged as though she wasn't the least bit surprised to find herself in Kat's parlor.

"What do you mean Dimitri's gone?" McAllister asked, dropping into a chair perpendicular to the sofa. "Gone where?"

"I told you, I don't know and I don't care. And can you please cross your legs or something?" Elle grumbled irritably and looked quickly at the ceiling. "He got what he needed from me. He knows how to find the *Fallen* who destroyed his family now, and if he had to break the heart of some freaky lab rat pseudo-angel in the process...oh, well...too bad, too sad, right?"

McAllister straightened in his chair. "Jebe? He found Jebe?"

"He goes by the name of Justin Chen now. You know, the money behind Gatewick's little operation."

"When did he find this out?" McAllister rose to his feet and came to stand in front of the women, looking down at Elle from his great height.

"Oh, c'mon, McAllister! Do you honestly expect me to believe you *Defensori* don't share this kind of information? Though, I have to admit both of you play dumb really well. Obviously, he saw something in my memories while he was taking care of me. As for my being an insecure little lab rat who just happened to be his bound mate...well, didn't that just make it all too freakin' easy?" Elle sneered making no attempt to hide the pain of betrayal.

"I take back my earlier assessment of your intelligence, lady. For a woman who's made a career of writing about love and romance, it's sad you don't even recognize it when it bites you in the ass. Dimitri Radchenko has more humanity and less deceit in his soul than any man I know, *Earthbound* or otherwise. He would never use you, or anyone else, for information. He would simply have asked."

"He didn't deny it!" Elle cried hotly, squirming under McAllister's accusatory gaze.

"He wouldn't. He would expect his mate, a woman who claimed to care for him, to recognize his true nature and give him the benefit of the doubt. An *Earthbound* can no more betray his bound mate than sign a pact with Lucifer."

"Well, how in the hell was I supposed to know that? I wasn't raised in a typical family environment or traditionally indoctrinated into this whole *Earthbound* lifestyle, you know."

An angry flush stained McAllister's face. He opened his mouth to continue the debate, but Kat held up her hand to stay his tongue.

"She's right, Kassian. Having been betrayed by someone she loved and trusted once, isn't it understandable she would jump to that conclusion again under the circumstances? Insecurity is a bitch." She took Elle's hand and turned in her seat to face her friend. "I get where you're coming from Elle. Honestly I do, but Dimitri loves you. Don't let stubbornness and pride get in the way of what your heart knows to be true. Now, at the moment, my empath senses my husband is more than a little concerned about Dimitri, so why don't you tell us exactly what happened?"

Elle felt the tight constriction in her chest ease as she related the evening's events. They were right. Dimitri did love her. She'd jumped to conclusions and let her past rise up and form a wall between them without giving him a chance to explain. He hadn't stormed out because he didn't care, he'd done it because he was hurt and angry she hadn't trusted in him, hadn't trusted in what they shared. He hadn't denied her accusations, but neither had he confirmed them. Maybe he'd left to give himself time to cool off and her time to stew in her own assumptions until she figured out she was a complete ass?

"That's probably part of it," McAllister allowed when Elle shared the thought with the two of them. "But my guess is he's gone hunting. Alone. I will, of course, kick his gigantic ass for that when I find him. But first I have to find him."

Without another word, McAllister stalked into the bedroom and slammed the door, presumably to get dressed. At least, Elle hoped he was going to get dressed. She'd had one too many free shows for the night. Though Dimitri had told her not to leave the apartment, it wasn't as though she'd done it deliberately, and waiting here with Kat…she was just as safe. Once McAllister found him? Then she would do whatever it took to convince him her lack of faith in herself, not her lack of faith in him, was the root of the problem. Maybe it wouldn't be quite as difficult now that she finally understood it herself.

"Coffee?" Kat rose gracefully to her feet. "Rhetorical question, of course."

McAllister picked that moment to stride from the

bedroom, dressed in black leather from head to toe. The hot glance Kat gave her husband as she headed past him into the kitchen spoke volumes. As for Elle, she was just happy there were now several layers of impenetrable fabric between her sight line and everything McAllister owned. She'd just opened her mouth to ask where he planned to start looking when she felt the color drain from her face and a sensation of cold dread snaked through her body.

"Dimitri," she whispered, knowing without a doubt that something had happened. She hadn't even been aware of the bond, but suddenly she couldn't feel him anymore. Instinctively, she knew they'd been connected somehow and now they weren't. She turned her stricken face up to McAllister who took one look at her expression and loosed a string of curses in several different languages that almost turned the air visibly blue.

Elle struggled to make sense of it while her heart pounded and her lungs strained to take in air. Gatewick was human and no match for Dimitri. Even Chen, assuming he was at the compound, was only one *Fallen,* and Dimitri was one extremely lethal pissed off angel with an agenda. How could either of them possibly have taken him down? Her mind quickly shuffled through one fact and possibility after another, quickly discarding each in turn. When the truth hit her, it did so with a suddenness that caused her to cry out in agony. She scrambled to her feet and clutched at McAllister's jacket, pulling his face down to hers.

"I know what they're doing. The experiments, the monthly injections, the retroviruses. Don't you see? I didn't grow into my powers. That's why they're coming back now. I always had them and was given something that suppressed them, something that was supposed to kill me but hadn't been perfected yet. My *creation* was a success, but that wasn't the ultimate goal. Dimitri said Jebe's goal was to exterminate the *Earthbound*. What better way than to develop a virus designed to infect and kill them? Oh God, McAllister, what if Gatewick finally figured it out? We have to find him before it's too late!"

"Son-of-a-bitch!" McAllister roared, grasping one of Elle's hands in his, and with the other reached for his wife, who'd hurried back into the room. Wrapping his arm around her, he pulled her to his side and kissed her hard. "I have to go. I'll call Galen and Alec on the way and have them meet me there. Kat, you call Luca. Tell him to get hold of Michael and let him know he needs to get over here. If Elle's right, and Jebe has been able to successfully develop something like that, we may need his help. Elle, if they manage to get here before we get back, you can give them directions to the compound, right?"

She nodded mutely. He squeezed her hand before releasing it.

"Okay, sit tight. We'll find him."

"Be careful, Kassian," Kat stretched up to kiss his cheek.

"Always am." He hugged her close and then released her before striding to the door and disappearing into thin air as soon as he was through the doorway and clear of the *sigils.*

Kat followed slowly behind him and quietly closed the door, leaning her forehead against it for just a moment and taking a deep breath before turning back to

Elle.

"How about you make the coffee while I call my brother?"

"How do you stand it, Kat? Every time he walks out the door you know what he could be walking into. How do you stay so calm?"

"Calm?" Kat's lips twisted in a comic imitation of a smile. "I'm nothing of the sort. But if he's distracted thinking I'm here worrying my head off, then that puts him in even more danger. So I paste on a smile and wave him on his way. I hate it. But I knew what I was getting into when I married him, and I wouldn't trade any of it for the alternative of living without him."

"Well, you sure had me fooled." Elle raised her brows.

"Good!" Kat's smile was tired but more genuine this time. "You know me as well as anyone. So if you bought it, maybe he did, too. Now go and make the coffee. It'll give you something to occupy your mind for five minutes while I call Luca. Dimitri is a *Defensori*, Elle. He's their brother. They won't come back without him."

"I know." And she did. The cold tendrils of fear churning in her gut and climbing into her chest to wrap icy fingers around her heart were because she was terrified the Dimitri they brought back would be nothing more than a lifeless body.

Chapter Seventeen

By the time Dimitri hunkered down in the bushes outside Gatewick's building, he'd managed to reign in his anger and look at the whole situation more objectively. Secure in his righteous indignation that she could consider him guilty for even a nanosecond, he'd stormed out of the apartment, fists clenched, chest tight, and snorting like a bull. But Elle's pale, stricken face stuck in his mind. He couldn't rid his conscience of those big blue eyes sparking defiance and begging for reassurance at the same time. Hell yeah, it cut like a knife that she could doubt him after everything they'd shared, after he'd let her into his mind and offered her his heart, but then he remembered this was a woman who, despite her outward confidence and swagger, harbored deep-seeded feelings of inadequacy. It wasn't something that would go away overnight. Was it really so surprising it would rear its ugly head when she felt uncertain or threatened? If her own father would betray her, why shouldn't she be suspicious of a man she'd only really known for a few months? Given her history, she probably couldn't help jumping to the conclusion she had, but he'd seen it in her face. She hadn't wanted to believe it, she'd wanted to believe in *him,* and he hadn't done anything to help her do that. He should have at least denied the accusation, should have stayed and talked to her. Instead, he'd stormed out assuming once she thought about it, she'd understand he refused to justify her finger pointing with an explanation because she should have known him better. In his haste to jump on the pride wagon, he'd managed to completely forget everything he knew about her and do exactly the wrong thing. Well, wasn't that freakin' special?

Dimitri slowly rose to his feet and stretched his tense muscles. What was he doing here, anyway? If this Chen really was Jebe, there was no reason to believe he would suddenly disappear tonight. Dimitri had waited seven hundred years, and he sure as hell could wait another day. Tonight Elle needed him more than he needed vengeance. It was time to go home. He'd hurt her. He realized that now. Sucking in a breath, he blew it out slowly. He didn't know much about groveling, but if that's what it was going to take to reassure her, he guessed he could give it a try. Of course, he'd make it very clear she should savor it as a one-time experience.

Dangerously preoccupied with thoughts of Elle, he failed to notice another mind in his vicinity seconds before he heard the crack of a rifle and felt the scalding pain. He reached for the spot instinctively and yanked a dart resembling a hypodermic needle from the side of his neck. Struggling to stay conscious long enough to fade out, he quickly worked a basic set of *sigils* around the nearest tree, squinting through the gray vortex engulfing him as a figure crashed through the underbrush in his direction, setting off a series of shocks along his spine. And then the world went black.

****

As he struggled up through the layers of darkness to consciousness, Dimitri was careful to give no indication he was once again aware of his surroundings. The hard, cold surface on which he lay was clearly concrete, and as his mind searched his immediate surroundings, he discovered he was not alone. A quick scan revealed his companion was human. A confused human who was pretty much scared to death of the circumstances he found himself in and the motionless, leather-clad giant now sharing his space. A complete scan provided more useful information. As Dimitri shuffled through the man's memories, he learned they were currently housed in a concrete and metal cell somewhere below Gatewick's cryogenic business. As he continued to examine the other man's recollection of the events leading up to his sojourn in captivity, Dimitri's eyes flew open and he jack-knifed into a sitting position.

"What in the hell are *you* doing here?" He growled.

Jim-by-the-way, aka Nerd-nuts, cowered further back into the corner of the cell, his teeth audibly chattering.

"I…I was sort of hoping you could tell me," he gasped, wide-eyed. "I was just minding my own business when these guys yanked me off my bike and into a van. They started asking me all kinds of questions about the woman at a house I'd been to. Hey, I'm just a fan who saw her on the bus and decided to take a chance. Believe me, I'm not usually a risk-taker, and now I know why."

"What did you tell them about Elle?" Dimitri rose to his feet, towering threateningly over the cringing man.

"Nothing! I didn't tell them anything. I figured they were reporters or something trying to get the scoop on her sabbatical. Of course, I can't see why reporters would bring me here and lock me up. I mean, Miss Gates is awesome and all, but c'mon…all this for an exclusive? Who are you, anyway? Oh, shoot! You're the boyfriend aren't you? She wasn't kidding about that whole over the top muscle thing. Look, I'm sorry man. I'll never bother her again. I swear."

Dimitri's eyes bored into the other man's as he read him. The poor schmuck was telling the truth. He was simply a rabid fan who'd gotten caught in the middle of something he couldn't even begin to imagine.

"If luck is on my side, I'm the guy who's going to get both of our asses out of here in one piece. So what *did* you tell them?"

"I told them I was a Jehovah's Witness sharing my mission and I didn't know who the woman at the house was, but she hadn't been especially interested in what I had to say."

"Quick thinking." Dimitri's lips curled in an unwilling smile. "They bought it?"

Jim shrugged. "Who knows? They didn't really seem to know what I was talking about, but they didn't let me go, either."

"Yeah, well they must have been *animorti*. Not a lot of brain cells firing in those guys," Dimitri rolled his eyes toward the ceiling, halting on the metal plates anchored there with heavy bolts. "Shit!"

"What's wrong? Aside from the obvious, I mean. And what are *animorti*?"

"You don't really want to know," Dimitri replied absently, unsnapping his sleeve and drawing a stiletto from the tattoo on his forearm, ignoring Jim's wide-eyed stare as the man curled up and tried to make himself even smaller. Stretching his arm over his head as high as he could, Dimitri drew the tip of his weapon along one of the plates, swearing again as sparks rained down on both men. Hell forged steel. No wonder Galen hadn't been able to get a read on the men he'd seen after they entered the building. The lower level must be lined with the stuff. Not only was it an effective block against *Earthbound* telepathy, it also prevented him from fading, flushing that means of escape right down the crapper. He was going to have to rely on Plan B. Just as soon as he came up with it.

"Do you know how many of them there are?" Dimitri dropped cross-legged to the floor.

"Well, there were the two who grabbed me and brought me here, then there was an Asian looking guy. He was here when I arrived but didn't stay long. Other than that, I just saw one older man who looked very uncomfortable with the whole thing," Jim said.

"How long have I been out?"

"Couple of hours."

"Must be close to morning." Elle would be alone and unprotected except for the *sigils* around his place. Hurt and alone, she would, of course, jump to the conclusion he wasn't coming back and then she would leave. She would stubbornly and impulsively walk right into danger and there wasn't a damn thing he could do to stop her. *Shit!* "Have they been feeding you?"

"The old guy brought me something to eat last night before the two who grabbed me threw you in here. Can't say I had much of an appetite, though. What do you think they intend to do with us?"

Dimitri was relatively sure they intended to kill both of them, but it wouldn't help Jim's obvious anxiety to share that little piece of information with him. Besides, Dimitri had no intention of going down without a fight, and he sure as hell wasn't letting an innocent bystander lose his life over an addiction to romance novels.

"Jim, I want you to listen to me. Whatever happens, whatever you see or hear, try not to react. I warn you, some of it is going to seem pretty far-fetched, but you need to stay cool. I'll get us out of here. Just keep your mouth shut, your head down, and follow my lead. No matter what. Got it?"

"I'll try."

"Trying isn't good enough. No matter how shocked or how scared you get, if I get distracted by you, we've got big problems."

"Because our lives depend on it?"

"Yeah, something like that."

"I have a hunch it's exactly like that. I'll try my best."

"Good man." Dimitri slapped him on the shoulder and a pained groan escaped Jim's lips as the color drained from his face. "What's the deal? I barely tapped you."

"It's my shoulder," Jim bit his lip hard enough to draw blood. "When they pulled me into the van…I think maybe it's dislocated."

"Let me have a look," Dimitri leaned forward as Jim shrank back, holding the injured arm stiffly at his side, slightly away from his body, and with the forearm turned outward.

"Uh, no that's okay."

"C'mon, man. I'm a doctor," Dimitri reached toward the injured shoulder.

"You don't look like a doctor," Jim gave Dimitri's long hair and leather-clad bulk a doubtful once over. "And if you really are a doctor, you should know all those steroids are no good for you."

"Yeah, I get that a lot." Dimitri grinned. "Now c'mon, let's see what we've got."

Supporting Jim's forearm with one hand, Dimitri gently probed the offending joint with the other. The muscles surrounding the shoulder were tightly spasmed with obvious swelling around the joint. The joint itself was squared off as opposed to a normal rounded appearance, and Jim sucked in a breath while beads of sweat popped out on his forehead as Dimitri palpated the head of the humerus bone clearly protruding in front.

"Yep, dislocated. I'm going to have to reduce it before the spasms get any worse."

"Reduce it?" Jim's voice quavered.

"Put it back in place. I won't lie. It's gonna hurt. But the longer we wait the harder it's gonna be."

"Could you remove my belt please?"

"Well gee, Jim…not sure I know you well enough." Dimitri grinned, attempting to distract and calm the man while he yanked the belt free of Jim's khaki's, folded it up, and shoved it between Jim's teeth. "Ready?"

Jim bit down hard on the leather, turned even paler, and after taking a deep breath, nodded slowly.

Holding the injured limb tightly against the man's body, Dimitri flexed Jim's elbow to a ninety-degree angle and gently rotated the shoulder outward. Jim sucked in a pained breath through his nose and locked his jaw on the belt. Dimitri continued to support the arm while waiting to see if the muscles were going to cooperate enough to allow the shoulder to spontaneously relocate. When that didn't happen, he gently lifted the arm above Jim's head, grunting in satisfaction as an audible and palpable clunk indicated the head of the humerus had returned to its normal anatomical position.

Jim tore the belt from between his teeth, his eyes wide with the sudden relief.

"Wow that feels a lot better!" He almost smiled as he followed Dimitri's directions to make a fist and wiggle his fingers. After ensuring there was no apparent nerve damage, Dimitri rolled up Jim's belt and shoved it in his pocket.

"We'll use this later for a sling. It's not ideal, but it's all we've got. For now, it's better if no one realizes you aren't in top form, so just hook your thumb in your belt loop to support the arm until we have another option."

"Thanks. Whatever you say, but frankly, I'm not sure my form is going to be of any use to you whether it's at the top or not." Jim dropped his eyes as his lips twisted in a self-deprecating expression.

"Well, not being a hindrance is its own way of being a help, okay?"

"Okay." Jim leaned back against the wall of the cell with a relieved sigh as Dimitri's head whipped around toward the metallic grating of a key being turned in a lock somewhere down the corridor. Given Jim's earlier observations and the fact that Dimitri felt no electrical shocks racing up and down his spine heralding the presence of evil, he assumed their imminent visitor could only be one man. One man he very much wanted to strangle with his bare hands.

Putting a finger to his lips, he moved stealthily toward the door as footsteps approached. The visitor had no sooner slid back the panel in the upper part of the door, revealing an opening to a hallway outside, than Dimitri's hand shot through and grabbed him by the throat. The tray of food clattered to the floor as the man clawed at the iron bands of the angel's fingers obstructing his windpipe.

"Please," the older man begged in a strangled whisper.

Dimitri stared impassively at the bug-eyed and quickly mottling face of John Gatewick, realizing for the first time in his many years of existence, he could take a human life with no remorse whatsoever. On some level, he realized it should bother him, but remembering what this man had put Elle through made it nearly impossible to feel guilt.

"Uh, hey. Doc? If you kill him now, we're still stuck in here and his friends won't be too happy to discover the body cooling outside the door," Jim offered in a calm tone.

"Yeah, good point," Dimitri acknowledged, loosening his grip just enough to allow Gatewick to gulp in a breath. "Okay, asshole, let's talk about your daughter."

Chapter Eighteen

"Have you lost your damned mind? It's out of the question." McAllister's tone of voice alone would have made most people back down, even without his dark frown and aggressive stance. But Elle had never been most people.

"I wasn't asking permission, McAllister, I was outlining my plan." Elle leaned toward the mirror and continued to apply the heavy layer of make-up which altered her appearance completely. Anxiety for Dimitri and fear of being caught in her nightmare ensured a long, sleepless night with plenty of time to think. With a final swipe of the brush over her cheeks, she bent to rummage through the bag Galen had been accommodating enough to retrieve from her apartment, earlier. Pulling free a long, black wig, she turned back to the mirror, tugging the wig down firmly over the flesh-tone skullcap currently concealing her natural brown locks. When she'd adjusted it to her satisfaction, she rose from Kat's vanity and turned to face the occupants of the room.

"What do you think?"

"You look like an Adams' family reject," McAllister grumbled.

"As long as I don't look anything like myself, Morticia's much younger and more attractive sister works for me." Elle sighed at the expression on Kassian

187

McAllister's face. He wasn't happy and was making no attempt to pretend otherwise. She really didn't want to antagonize her best friend's husband, but no one else had been able to think of a way into the compound, and the longer they debated, the greater the risk to Dimitri. "So which one of you big strong *Earthbound* wants to be my baby daddy?"

"I told you, you are not doing this. First of all, Dimitri would kick my ass if I allowed you to put yourself in danger this way, and secondly it will never work," McAllister replied in a tone that didn't invite debate.

Elle's nostrils flared as she stalked across the room, bringing herself toe to toe with the much larger man. She planted her fists on her hips and looked up at him through the thick coat of mascara tangling her lashes like spider's legs. Combined with the heavy layer of eyeliner, she ran a real risk of sealing her eyes closed every time she blinked.

"Sorry to burst your macho bubble, but I'm not asking your permission. If we don't get him out of there, Dimitri won't be around to kick anyone's ass."

Swallowing the palpitations climbing into her throat, she firmly ignored the churning nausea swirling in her gut ever since the men had returned with the news they'd found Dimitri's *sigils* indicating he'd been taken.

He'd stormed out of his apartment thinking she believed the worst of him. She'd been a fool to discount everything her heart and soul told her to be true before she'd discovered the painting. And she would tell the big lug that very thing right to his face. Just as soon as she found him. Her plan would work. It had to. She needed to believe it, even if no one else did. Failure was simply not an option. She lifted her chin a fraction higher before continuing in a tight voice, "Look, if Galen is right about this microchip in my wrist, I'm our ticket in. I don't know why it didn't occur to me sooner, but that has to be what it is. I never had to enter any kind of code or anything when I came home from classes or when I moved about between the living quarters and the lab. Yet, it stands to reason there has to be some kind of security in place, right? And if we're wrong? Nothing ventured, nothing gained. Besides, I don't see anyone else coming up with a better plan. I can't just sit around here doing nothing while Dimitri is in danger."

"I would do the same thing if it were you, Kassian," Kat said quietly, laying a hand on her husband's visibly tense forearm and stroking it soothingly with her fingertips. "You know I would."

"If you think reminding me you have the capacity to be just as reckless as your friend is going to help matters, Katrina, you're sadly mistaken." McAllister glared at his wife, the first time that Elle had ever seen him look at her with anything other than complete adoration. "And there isn't a man here who would let you risk yourself like that."

"There isn't a man here who could stop me if your life was on the line, any more than anyone could stop you if I was the one at risk," Kat shot back, silver eyes flashing dangerously.

"One has nothing to do with the other," he growled.

"Oh?" Kat arched a brow. "I *know* you aren't going to say it's because you're a man and I'm not. You *aren't* going to go *there* are you, McAllister?" McAllister continued to glare down at her from beneath lowered brows, shaking his arm free as his wife's eyes narrowed to slits and golden sparks spurted from her fingertips. Elle wrinkled her nose as the stench of burnt hair rose into her nostrils.

"Okay, enough." Elle stepped between them, holding up her hands. "Look, I appreciate where you're coming from McAllister, but turn your boiling machismo down to simmer for a sec and look at this logically. You said yourself something is blocking all of you from getting a read on what's going on below ground, and whatever it is also prevents you from fading in. I know that place like the back of my hand. I know the layout, I know the way the operation works, and I likely have the key to unlocking the door planted right here in my arm. I understand you don't like the idea, but I'm the best chance we have for getting Dimitri back. Now, I can do this with your help, which is probably the safer and smarter route, or I can do it solo. Either way, I'm doing it. So what's it going to be?"

"You knew the layout several years ago." McAllister scrubbed a hand over his jaw. "What if you're way off base? Anything could have changed since then."

"Possibly. But if we don't try, we don't know. Right?" Turning to Galen, she held out her hand. "Were you able to hack in and get the consent forms and the FAQs so we have some idea what the hell we are supposed to be doing?"

"Piece of cake," the shiny-domed giant replied, opening a manila folder, extracting several sheets of paper and handing them to her. Elle barely glanced at them, gripping them tightly in her trembling hands and blowing out a long, slow breath. "Not only that, but just as I'd hoped, their closed circuit security cameras have remote access capability. Whoever set up the system didn't even bother to change the factory defaults for the username and password. I mean, you'll find that to be true about seventy percent of the time, but I would have expected someone with Gatewick's agenda to use a little more caution."

"Bottom line, Galen. Were you able to hack in so the cameras can be set on a loop?"

"Piece of cake," he repeated. "Once you're inside, I hit a button and instant déjà vu. Hopefully, I got them all."

"Hopefully. Okay, then. The only thing left is to decide who's volunteering to be the lucky sperm donor?"

"I'll do it," Alec said at last with a shrug. "I mean, I'm the most logical choice, right? You're known in the city Kass, and if they've been watching any of you for any length of time, it's possible they've seen Galen, too. Luca and Michael won't be here in time, and if Elle's suspicions are correct, we can't afford to wait. I've been out of the country for months. I'm the one they're least likely to recognize."

"I still don't like it," McAllister bit out, snaking an arm around his wife and hauling her against him. Kat's wide eyes were fixed on Elle. Given her empathic gift, Kat was probably the only person in the room who realized Elle's cocky bravado was an act and the prospect of stepping back onto Gatewick's turf nearly paralyzed her with fear. Kassian McAllister might not like the idea, but he couldn't possibly like the idea less than Elle.

Elle offered Alec McAllister a grateful smile and began shuffling through the papers Galen had provided. Waiting until Alec shrugged on one of his brother's sport coats, she handed him half the sheaf. He scanned the top one quickly, his dark brows drawing together in a frown.

"I hope you're a quick study. These are some of the questions couples looking to transfer their embryos from one facility to another might ask. Those who've struggled with infertility and suffered through a gamut of tests and procedures to get to this point are extremely protective of those little vials containing their best hope for a family. They'll have done their homework. If we're going to pull this off, we need to make sure it looks as though we've done ours."

"Got it." Alec glanced up from under his lashes and flashed his dimples in what should have been a reassuring grin, but Elle didn't relax one iota. Was it really mere days ago she believed she was strong enough to walk away from everyone and everything? Yet even as she'd mourned the impending loss of her life, her career, her best friend, even then, before she'd realized exactly what he meant to her, somewhere deep down she'd wanted Dimitri to stop her. Wanted him to want her. And he did. And how did she repay him? She'd thrown his love in his face and accused him of using her. She'd pushed him away and right out the door into the clutches of the enemy. One hand curled into a fist at her side while the other absently massaged her sternum, trying to ease the dull ache that had been a constant companion since the moment she'd felt

Dimitri's absence. The white silk blouse shifted softly against her skin, reminding her of the brush of Dimitri's hair and the whisper of his lips caressing her flesh and the ache became even more pronounced. For him, she willingly walked back through the gates of her own personal nightmare. For him, she would risk everything because now, without him, everything else was emptiness. Hell no, she couldn't relax. Knowing the consequences of failure, there were moments she feared her heart would actually stop, moments she could barely breathe.

"Elle?" Kat said quietly. "Honey, are you sure about this? You don't have to go back there. We can find another way."

Surprised to realize she'd been lost in thought and they were all watching her closely, Elle's head snapped up. She swallowed hard, flipped her temporary identity's black hair over one shoulder, and straightened her spine. She stared each of them directly in the eye in turn.

"Thanks, Kat, but you're wrong. I do have to go back there. Now, if you're ready, Alec, let's get this freak show on the road, shall we?"

****

As Gatewick gasped out his story, Dimitri's fingers loosened until they were barely tight enough to maintain a grip on the man.

"Do you honestly expect me to believe that load of shit?" Dimitri spat.

"It's the truth, I swear," Gatewick croaked. If the fool was to be believed, everything he'd ever done had been to protect Elle. Well, hadn't he done a bang up freakin' job?

"Drop your shields and I'll decide whether it's the truth or not," Dimitri demanded in a steely voice. Gatewick nodded painfully and opened his mind. As Dimitri explored every thought and memory, every hidden fear, his grip loosened completely and his fingers curled into a fist as the man collapsed to the floor gasping.

"Do you have any idea what she's suffered because of you?" He growled.

"Better she hate me and escape," Gatewick whispered hoarsely. "Chen will never give up trying to eradicate the *Earthbound*. Procrastination was the best I could do to keep us both alive as long as I have. He'll figure out the truth eventually, but at least Arabella won't be here to suffer his wrath. I'm resigned to paying for my stupidity with my own life but I'll be damned if I'll sacrifice hers."

"Why didn't you just tell her the truth?"

"Considering you were about to kill me on her behalf, I assume you know Arabella fairly well." Gatewick coughed, massaging his throat and climbing slowly to his feet. "If that's the case, surely you realize if I told her the truth, she never would have left. She would have believed she could outsmart Chen and save me."

"So instead you let her believe she was created in vitro to serve as a guinea pig? Well, you might have succeeded in making her hate *you*, old man, but you made damn sure she's spent the last years hating *herself* just as much."

"That was never my intention, and it's unfortunate, but she's alive isn't she? It was imperative Chen never realize her true nature. If he suspected for a minute, she *would* have been fodder for experimentation. That or he would have simply killed her outright as he threatened to do every time I objected to anything he wanted. How do you think he kept me in line all these years? The only way to ensure her safety was to do whatever it took to drive her away once she was old enough to take care of herself and then make him believe I was glad to see her go."

"So how *did* he find out the truth? Someone sent *animorti* looking for her. I gather it wasn't you?"

"He still doesn't know the truth. But he's never stopped looking for her. She's always been his leverage, you see, and I think he was afraid I would refuse to cooperate unless he could use her against me. He never realized I continued to cooperate to lessen his urgency to find her. He's had the phone lines in and out of this place bugged for years, so when she called…"

"He managed to narrow the search area. That's how you knew where to send the letter," Dimitri finished in a grim tone.

"Exactly."

"If he knew where she was, why didn't he just grab her?"

"He decided he didn't want her getting in the way or finding out too much. It was enough that he made sure I knew he could do so at any time."

"When do you expect him back?"

"Back? Oh, he hasn't left. He's over in my library enjoying a brandy and gloating over having captured a *Defensori*. The entire lab complex is laced with Hell forged steel and the living quarters are separate, which is why you probably can't feel him. My assignment was to create a retro-virus designed to kill *Earthbound*. His plan is to have me inject you to confirm the efficacy and then develop a distribution plan to infect you all."

"So we'll have you to thank for our ultimate annihilation?"

"Of course not," Gatewick's lips curled derisively. "But Chen doesn't know that. Oh, he'll find out eventually and then he'll kill me, but at least I'll be the one paying for my naiveté."

"What are you talking about?"

"I'd been quite happily conducting independent genetic research when my brother and his wife, Arabella's parents, were murdered. Ambushed in a cheap motel and stabbed to death. My sister-in-law was *Earthbound*, so I knew *Fallen* had to have been involved for a knife wound to take her life."

"Hellblade?"

"One would assume. Chen approached me out of the blue shortly after their deaths and offered to provide unlimited financial backing for both my cryogenics business and my own personal research. That's a carrot any scientist will bite if you dangle it in his face. Chen also claimed to be *Earthbound* himself, someone who was working against the *Fallen*. As a human, I couldn't feel his evil and had no way of knowing the truth. I saw it as an opportunity to avenge the death of my brother and his wife. I began to suspect the truth when Chen told me of his lifelong quest to discover the whereabouts of a deadly poison that could destroy anyone or anything evil it touched—human, demon, or *Fallen*. I knew exactly what it was, of course."

"The Ampule of Tears," Dimitri let out a long slow breath. "Damn Michael and his youthful indiscretions. How did Chen get his hands on it?"

"He didn't. My brother had been a *Librarian.* Centuries ago, the Order had obtained the ampule from one of Aandalena's descendants, who wisely decided it was far too dangerous to be out in general circulation. When Lawrence left the Order to marry, the ampule was entrusted to him and his *Earthbound* wife for safe-keeping. The *Librarians* figured it was better to transfer it out of their possession lest someone discover its existence and begin to question their claims of neutrality."

"Why the hell didn't they just give it back to Michael and take it out of circulation permanently?" Dimitri spat.

"I don't know, but again I would reference their concerns of being perceived as having taken one side over the other. Anyway, as soon as Chen mentioned it, I understood. I also understood why Lawrence and Penny had died. Why they'd left Arabella on my doorstep and gone on the run. They'd tucked the ampule in with her things along with a note explaining what it was and that I was to keep it out of *Fallen* hands at all cost. I knew then exactly what Chen was and that my family had died by his hand. He was hoping to acquire the poison and bastardize it into something that would kill *Earthbound* instead of *Fallen*. Failing that, he'd bought himself a scientist to create a virus to do it. But by the time I figured it all out, he had me by the balls. All he needed to do was threaten Arabella, who he believed was *my* daughter. She was just a baby at the time, so I had little choice but to play along if I wanted to keep her safe."

"So you've actually been working against him all these years?"

"Not overtly perhaps, but in my own small way. My first priority was to ensure he never found out the truth about Arabella, that she was actually half *Earthbound*. Instead of a means to destroy the *Earthbound*, I initially used Chen's money to develop a virus that temporarily inhibits *Earthbound* powers. It required periodic injections to maintain the virus at a level that ensured the abilities remained completely suppressed, but it allowed me to keep Arabella's true nature hidden for years. Instead of fairy tales and bedtime stories, I told her about the *Earthbound* and the *Librarians*, hoping that if she ever managed to escape, she would seek them out and learn the truth about her parents and who she was. Are her powers returning?"

Dimitri nodded shortly.

"Good. I had no idea what the cumulative effects of the virus might be. I did have concerns that after so many years of the booster shots I might have..." Gatewick swallowed hard. "Well, anyway, while Chen believed I was working on *his* goal, I was really working on my own. Development of a retrovirus whose genetic code could be manipulated to infect *him* with the poison in the vial, spread it to the other *Fallen*, and kill them all."

"And?"

"Haven't even come close," Gatewick shook his head slowly. "That's not how the poison was designed to work and because it was created supernaturally, it doesn't conform to the laws of science."

"Where's the ampule now?"

Dimitri felt the color leave his face as Gatewick dug into the pocket of his pants and held up a small, golden vial encrusted with gemstones.

"You've been carrying the damn thing around with you all these years? Don't you think that's just a little irresponsible, all things considered?" Dimitri growled.

"Well, perhaps it would be if it contained anything more harmful than a simple saline solution," Gatewick offered Dimitri a conspiratorial grin. "With the exception of the tiny sample I extracted to work with, which I destroyed when I was unable to convert it, I transferred the original contents to another receptacle years ago. It's securely tucked away in a safe deposit box in Lucerne. I figured if Chen ever discovered Lawrence had passed the ampule to me and was able to get his hands on it, the only thing he'd stand to gain would be a pretty little bottle worth nothing more than its weight in gold."

"Well, when this is all over, we'll need to retrieve the original substance and return it to Michael. In the meantime, don't worry. You won't need the poison or a virus to kill the bastard. I'll be more than happy to take care of that for you with my own two hands."

Chapter Nineteen

"Maybe you should have used a little more war-paint. You're pale as a ghost," Alec cracked as he handed Elle from the back of the limo.

Gripping his fingers tightly enough to fracture bone, Elle glanced nervously at the camera above the entrance to the facility and smoothed a palm down the side of her navy wool jacket before tugging the hem into place.

"Yeah, well, I feel like one. This isn't a visit I ever thought I'd be making," she answered while privately crowning herself the Queen of Understatement. "If this whole plan goes due south, you *can* get us out of here, right?"

"In a heartbeat, sweetness. Now try to look like a woman who's concerned with nothing in the world beyond the safe relocation of her cryogenically frozen potential bundles of joy, okay?" Alec grinned, slipping an arm around Elle's shoulders and gently steering her toward the entrance.

Elle stiffened and shuffled along beside him trying not to drag her feet in the three-inch heels.

"And it probably wouldn't hurt if you acted as though you actually liked me a little since we are supposed to be a crazy in love young couple desperate to have a child. Loosen up, kiddo."

"I *do* like you Alec and I *am* crazy in love, it just

happens to be with someone else," Elle retorted sharply, then blew out a breath and lifted her chin determinedly. "I'm sorry, it's this place. I can do this, really. I just needed a minute to get myself together. This isn't exactly a case of John-Boy coming home to Walton's Mountain, you know. Being here doesn't exactly give me the warm fuzzies. I'm ready now. Let's start the dog and pony show."

Alec kept a firm grip on her as he reached for the tinted glass door with Gatewick Cryogenic Sperm and Embryo Storage written in small, white block letters. A flock of butterflies rising into her throat, Elle remembered Dimitri's instructions and did her best to discreetly breathe in through her nose and out through her mouth without looking like a panting dog. Rivulets of sweat trickled down between her breasts as the door whooshed closed behind them and she blinked rapidly. She looked around like a wild animal caught in a trap as she waited for her eyes to adjust to the dim interior.

The lobby reeked of expensive elegance with sleek modern furnishings in shades of teal and brown and thick, plush carpeting as opposed to the standard commercial grade. Classical piano music tinkled faintly in the background. The only other sound disturbing the stillness was the sharp staccato of the receptionist's nails on the computer keyboard on the counter in front of her. She looked up brightly as they approached the desk, moved the laptop she'd been working on to the side, and stood to greet them. About Elle's height, with golden blonde hair pulled into a tight knot at the nape of her neck, she exuded cool competence. She was also a complete stranger. Elle released a restrained sigh of relief. The woman hadn't been employed when Elle was here, therefore she was unlikely to recognize her, disguise or not. The blonde held out a hand, first to Elle and then to Alec, lingering over Alec's a little longer than Elle thought was strictly professional.

"Good morning and welcome to Gatewick Cryogenics. I'm Yvonne. How can I help you today?"

Elle opened her mouth to speak, pausing to clear her throat when no sound was immediately forthcoming. "Hello. I'm Jennie Barrow and this is my husband Alec. We're relocating from the West Coast and we're interested in transferring our embryos to a location nearby," Elle said in a voice that sounded shaky even to her own ears.

"You'll have to excuse my wife," Alec offered his most charming smile complete with dimples. "This whole infertility issue has been very difficult for us both. This will be our second move in three years and the last time we transferred embryos…well, let's just say it didn't go very well. We're both more than a little nervous about doing it again. Still, it's not really feasible to fly cross country for implantation."

"I understand completely," Yvonne responded in a mechanically soothing voice as she moved from behind the counter and gestured toward a small furniture grouping across from the reception desk indicating Elle and Alec should precede her. "I'm so sorry about your previous experience. I can assure you Gatewick has an excellent track record with transfers and we work very closely with the transferring facility to ensure everything goes smoothly. What can I tell you to help put your mind at ease?"

"Well," Elle began with deliberate hesitance. "Can you tell us a little about Gatewick's overall process for embryo transfer?"

"Of course," Yvonne smiled. "Well, first of all, you don't need to do a thing. Gatewick Cryogenic will arrange every detail. Once your completed embryo storage contract and paperwork is received, we will contact your current storage facility and schedule the transfer of your embryos to Gatewick."

"And how exactly does the transfer occur?" Alec leaned forward in the micro-suede club chair that was comically inadequate for a man of his size, propping his elbows on his knees and favoring the woman with an intensely earnest look. Elle gave him props for his acting skills. He really appeared to be deeply concerned about the fate of his fictitious unborn children.

"All embryos are shipped in liquid nitrogen dry shipper tanks and transported via private courier. The dry shipper tanks keep the embryos frozen for seven days from the date shipped but that's simply a precaution as all shipments within the United States are sent using priority overnight delivery." Yvonne reached a beautifully manicured hand to select a brochure from a plexi-glass holder on the small chrome and glass table next to her chair and held it out to Elle. "I think you'll find all of the information you're looking for in here, but of course I'm happy to answer any questions or address any concerns you may have."

When Elle continued to grip her hands together in her lap and stare at the pamphlet as though it had teeth, Alec reached for it instead and flipped it open. His dark brows knit together as he scanned the contents, and Elle couldn't help noticing the appreciative glances Yvonne was sneaking in his direction. Elle pressed her lips together tightly. Okay, so maybe she and Alec weren't actually a couple, and maybe he was extremely pleasant to look at—okay, he was freakin' stunning—but Blondie had no way of knowing they weren't happily married and her obvious interest annoyed Elle on principle alone. Of course, Alec could read the woman even better than Elle could and if he could successfully distract the woman by feigning interest, it would certainly work in their favor. With a pointed look at her 'husband,' Elle reached over and plucked the brochure from Alec's fingers.

"We'll have to look it over and get back to you," She snapped, jumping to her feet.

"Of course," the woman replied smoothly while rising gracefully to her feet. "Let me just assure you our facilities are equipped with the latest technology. Embryos are stored in state of the art vapor phase liquid nitrogen tanks. This area of the Northeast takes some heavy hits from ice storms in the winter so it's imperative we're not dependent on electricity to keep embryos frozen. Our cutting edge technology provides for the storage of specimens in the vapor phase one hundred percent of the time and our storage tanks are monitored twenty-four hours a day, seven days a week. The safety of your embryos is as important to us as it is to you."

"I doubt that," Elle snapped.

"Well, of course I only meant…" the blonde stammered.

"I'm sorry," Elle lied, closing her eyes and pinching the bridge of her nose between her thumb and forefinger, hoping she looked suitably contrite. "This whole process…well, it's just very stressful. Especially after…" Elle broke off in a choked voice, sniffling softly and swiping at the corners of her eyes.

"I understand completely," Yvonne assured them in a slightly cooler voice.

"We appreciate your time." Alec rose to his feet and slung a beefy arm around Elle's shoulders, gave her a squeeze, then held out his other hand to Yvonne. "We'll look over the information and get back to you later in the week, but it certainly sounds as though Gatewick Cryogenic offers everything we're looking for."

"I'm sorry, but before we leave, do you have a ladies' room I could use?" Elle asked.

"I told you to go before we left home," Alec teased.

"Bladder the size of a lima bean, I'm afraid." Elle offered the receptionist an apologetic smile.

"Of course. Just down the hall there, take the first left." Yvonne smiled briefly at Elle and then turned the full force of her professionally enhanced smile on Alec.

"You know I can read your mind, right?" Elle heard Alec's amused voice in her head and her gaze snapped in his direction.

"Yeah, well then you know I think Blondie missed her calling...maybe she should rethink her career choice. She'd make a great Santa since she's got the ho-ho-ho part down pat." Elle thought back sourly, Alec's deepening dimple confirmed she'd successfully sent the thought back to him. Her heart leapt at the realization that if she could now communicate telepathically with Alec, then surely she could do the same to find Dimitri once she managed to disable the security. Assuming she actually *could* disable the security.

"Remember what we discussed. Find the door, locate the scanner, see if the chip gives you access, and then get your ass right back out here. No deviations from the plan, Elle. Got it?"

"Absolutely. Got it. No deviations. You just play nice with your new girlfriend while I check it out. Gotta go and pretend pee now, buh-bye."

Elle stretched up to peck Alec's cheek like a good "wife", and offered him her most dazzling smile. "I'll be right back, *darling*."

"Don't make me come looking for you, *sweetheart*," he warned in a teasing voice Elle knew was for Yvonne's benefit alone. The message he conveyed to Elle with a look was anything but lighthearted.

Elle tuned out Alec's flirtatious banter as she hurried down the hallway as familiar to her as her own reflection in the mirror. Quickly passing the doorways of the tastefully appointed restrooms provided for the use of the center's clients, she yanked open the door marked 'Private' at the end of the hallway, slipped inside, and pulled it closed behind her with a muted click. Leaning back against the door to support legs turned to rubber, Elle closed her eyes and waited for the blood pounding in her ears to quiet. Blowing out a long breath through pursed lips, she looked around the small vestibule and was hit with a serious case of déjà vu. To the left was the door that opened to a tunnel leading to her old home, her old life, the endless years of lies and subterfuge. Her chest tightened at the realization Gatewick's betrayal still had the power to hurt her. It was unexpected, but she supposed she shouldn't be surprised. When you discover the only family you have in the world regards you as nothing more than a clinical specimen, a means to an end, it damn well *should* hurt. Elle swallowed hard and swiped a finger under each eye. Enough. She was here to free Dimitri, not kiss and make up with the man who created her. That ship hadn't just sailed, she'd jumped in a lifeboat and paddled off in the opposite direction a long time ago.

To the right was the door behind which was the steep, metal staircase leading down to her father's laboratory. A red light blinked on the ceiling mounted camera over the entrance. She hoped Galen knew what he was doing so anyone who happened to be watching the monitors would see nothing but a continuous loop of an empty vestibule. She knew the lab was where they would be holding Dimitri, and she moved toward the door while examining the area around it for any type of electronic device. Her heart sank when she noticed nothing out of the ordinary, but then as she looked more closely, she noticed the small black strip running along the doorframe next to the latch. Hardly daring to hope, she reached for the handle and grasped it, which placed the chip in her wrist right near the strip. She gasped aloud as she detected a faint series of clicks followed by a muted beep. Holding her breath, she gave the handle a tentative tug, amazed and relieved as the latch gave way and the door opened easily.

According to the plan, Elle was supposed to leave the door slightly ajar, rejoin Alec in the lobby, and beat a hasty retreat. McAllister and Galen, and anyone else they'd been able to round up, were on stand-by less than a hundred yards away awaiting the signal to move in. That was the plan. She knew it was the plan. But all good intentions of sticking to the plan evaporated when she felt Dimitri's presence like the gentle brush of a spring breeze invading her consciousness. He was alive and he was close. To hell with the plan. What if someone discovered the door unlatched before the *Defensori* ever arrived? They might never get another chance. She was here *now* and though she hadn't often been allowed access to her father's lab, she still knew the layout better than anyone else. It was up to her. She would find Dimitri on her own before the others even realized she'd deviated from the plan. And if Gatewick or anyone else tried to stop her, well… she'd worry about that if and when the time came. Slipping her expensive stilettos off, she gripped them like a weapon in one hand and grasped the cold iron handrail with the other. Drawing and holding a deep breath, she glance up at the surveillance camera one last time before creeping forward and soundlessly descending the poorly illuminated metal stairs on trembling legs and stocking feet into her own personal hell.

Illuminated by the soft blue glow of the computer monitors standing sentinel along the black counter on the far wall, the microscopes, centrifuges, and steadily humming freezers and refrigeration units were unattended. Having half expected to come face to face with Gatewick, Elle breathed a quick sigh of relief upon finding the lab empty.

She'd just reached the bottom of the stairs and placed one nylon clad foot on the cold floor when Alec's voice shouted in her head before being abruptly cut off as the door clicked shut above her. A strange prickling sensation crept up her spine from her tailbone to the nape of her neck, an odd, uncomfortable feeling unlike anything she'd ever experienced before. She closed her eyes and swallowed the bile scalding the back of her throat while her legs began to shake in earnest. Her heart plummeted to her feet as she suddenly remembered that girl. That girl in every romantic suspense she'd ever written. That girl who made horror movie fans scream a warning from the comfort of their theater seat as she foolishly ventured into the basement or the attic or the darkened bedroom, never bothering to turn on a light. Good Lord, she was that girl! That stupid, stupid girl who dove in first and checked the depth of the water later. That girl who usually wound up dead. Curling her fingers even more tightly into the toes of her pumps, she grimly put one foot in front of the other and started across the polished concrete floor of the lab, ignoring the little voice screaming a warning in her head that someone or something was coming down the stairs behind her.

"You're safer in here. Just stay put and stay quiet until I come back for you," Dimitri told Jim, stepping out into the hallway with Gatewick.

"Look, Doc… I know I don't look very strong, but I like to think I'm fairly intelligent. Maybe there's something I can do to help." Jim braced his back against the wall and pushed himself to his feet. With a pained expression, he carefully used his good arm to guide his opposite hand in hooking his thumb in his belt loop to support his injured shoulder as Dimitri had directed. While Dimitri admired the guy's pluck, if his pasty complexion and the rivulets of sweat pouring down his face were any indication, he was far more likely to pass out cold and simply get underfoot than provide any real assistance no matter how noble his intentions.

"Appreciate it, buddy, but I think you'd better stay here. I'll call you if I need you, okay?"

"What if I don't hear you?"

"You'll hear me." Dimitri sent the thought into the other man's mind and Jim's eyes widened.

"You weren't kidding!" Jim gulped audibly.

"About?"

"The risk of seeing or hearing things that might seem far-fetched."

"Kid, you ain't seen nothing yet." Dimitri grinned and started to swing the door closed. Suddenly he froze as shocks raced up and down his spine. He'd been expecting that. What was completely unexpected, what stopped him in his tracks and sent his heart racing into a full out gallop, was the warm sensation of awareness brushing his consciousness almost simultaneously. What the hell? *"Elle?"*

Chapter Twenty

Elle dropped her shoes with a clatter and grabbed for the nearest countertop, sending a rack of empty test tubes to the floor with a crash, as her knees buckled in relief at the sound of Dimitri's voice in her head. *So much for stealth*, she thought ruefully as she carefully picked her way around the shattered shards of glass and bent to retrieve her shoes. She still wasn't sure how the whole telepathy thing worked, so she simply opened her mind and hoped her thoughts somehow reached him.

"Dimitri? Oh thank God! Where are you? I'm here!"

"GET OUT!" He roared in her head. Elle gasped aloud and forcibly swallowed down a knot of hurt. Well, of course she'd known he was mad as hell when he stormed out, but surely, he must have some idea of what coming here had cost her? Staying angry when she was here facing down her most hellacious demons to save his sorry ass was just plain rude! She barely had time to consider a scathing response designed to guilt the big lug into an appropriately apologetic state when she felt a whisper of hot breath on the back of her neck right before an arm snaked around her chest. *Well, shit!* Maybe Dimitri hadn't been angry with her after all. Maybe he'd been trying to warn her.

"Um, help?" Elle sent the thought instinctively,

211

though she knew Dimitri was unable to come to her aid. She remembered feeling the strange prickling sensation and attributing it to nerves. *Hmm, maybe not.* Then again, she'd never had it before so how was she supposed to recognize it? She really needed to have to have a long talk with her *Earthbound* friends about what to expect moving forward since her genetically engineered DNA was clearly evolving. Of course, in order to have that conversation, first she needed to survive. Elle forced herself to focus on the immediate problem. She'd gotten herself into this mess and it was increasingly apparent she was going to have to figure out a way to get herself out of it. And then she would rescue Dimitri.

"Well, well, well. Who do we have here?" Elle stiffened against the arm holding her in place, immediately recognizing the silky, well-modulated voice of Justin Chen. The hollow, measured echo of footsteps on metal indicated he was descending the stairwell behind her. She realized he must have been somewhere in the compound all along, because Alec and the others would never have allowed him to get past them if he'd simply walked in the front door. Damn, damn, and double damn! She tentatively arched against the man holding her, and was rewarded by the tightening of his forearm and a rough and painful squeeze of her breast.

"Hey, no touchy-feely, asshole!" Vaguely aware of heavy footsteps pounding in her direction from the maze of hallways and storerooms through the doorway at the back of the lab, Elle knew it had to be Gatewick. Well, she wasn't going down without a fight. Using her free hand to pry her captor's fingers loose, she flexed her knee and brought the heel of her foot down on his instep with as much force as she could muster. He grunted in pain and his arm loosened just enough for Elle to bring her arm up and launch an elbow backwards into his gut. As he doubled over and his arm fell away completely, Elle spun on her heel and swung her shoes directly at his head. One wickedly sharp stiletto heel caught him squarely in the temple and sank in with a sickening *thwack*. With a wide-eyed look of horror, the *animorti* exploded, spattering Elle and anything within a three-foot range, with a fine spray of stinking black goo, before settling into a slimy puddle at her feet.

Well, that was…unexpected. And gross. Elle had simply been hoping to knock the guy off balance long enough to scoot behind the nearest counter and put some distance between herself and Chen. She glanced down at her clothes. The white silk blouse she'd borrowed from Kat dripped with the slime, and the navy suit was trashed. Perhaps she could claim it as payback for the Louboutins? Distracted by the astonishing demise of the *animorti*, Elle never saw Chen move. Her heart dropped to her feet as he hooked an arm around her neck and tangled his other hand in her hair. Her shoes clattered to the floor as her hands flew to the top of her head to hold the wig in place, hoping he hadn't yet recognized her. Holding her in front of him like a shield, he whipped around to face the back of the lab as the door crashed open with a force that tore it from its hinges.

Even if she hadn't been looking, Elle would have recognized Dimitri by the feral growl rumbling up from the depths of his chest. She sagged against Chen in relief at the sight of him. He was alive, unharmed, and livid. Thankfully, it was directed at someone other than her for the moment. Her sense of relief was short-lived, however, as John Gatewick stepped up and around him.

"Dimitri, behind you!" She cried out.

"Let her go, Chen," Gatewick demanded. "I have what you want."

"That's where you're wrong, John," Chen hissed over her shoulder, so close to her ear that the uncomfortable sensation racing up and down her spine spread throughout her body, leaving her nerve endings buzzing. "I thought you had what I wanted, but I see now I've wasted endless years and tons of money on someone whose talents are far less extraordinary than I was led to believe. First Lawrence, and now you. The Gatewicks have been a disappointment to me on all counts."

"Perhaps. Perhaps not," Gatewick responded and glanced up at Dimitri with a secretive smile while reaching a hand into his pants pocket. Elle looked away from the man who'd raised her and let her eyes roam hungrily over Dimitri. If she was about to die, she wanted her last memory to be of him. Then the corner of his lips twitched and his eyelid flicked in a quick but unmistakable wink.

"Baby, I can't get a clear shot with you in front of him. As soon as Gatewick tosses the vial and Chen goes for it, you've got to move, got it?"

"Yes, but what...?" Clearly, Dimitri had a plan, and her father was in on it. It made no sense to her whatsoever, but if it had the potential to eliminate Chen and get Dimitri out of here in one piece, she was on board.

"Just move. And by the way, when this is all over I am so putting you over my knee for getting yourself in the middle of this." His tone was light, but the tight set of his jaw told Elle they weren't out of the woods yet. He was just trying to ease her fears. Well, she could do the same for him.

"Promise?" She waggled her brows suggestively.

Dimitri coughed and adjusted his stance just as Gatewick pulled his hand from his pocket and raised it in the air with a triumphant expression. Clutched in his fist was a small golden vial encrusted with gemstones and Chen sucked in a breath. The arm around her neck twitched while the grip on her hair tightened and pulled. Elle held the wig in place with a death grip.

"Where did you get that?" Chen croaked hoarsely.

"Why, I've had it for years, Justin," John Gatewick replied in a scathing tone. "If it makes you feel any better, you were on the right track. Lawrence and Penny *did* have the ampule, but I fear you must have tipped your hand, *old friend*. Before you killed them, my brother and his wife left both the ampule and their daughter with me for safekeeping."

"*Their* daughter?" Chen sputtered. "All these years…I never even suspected…she never exhibited any sign…"

"No, I made sure of that," Gatewick responded in a hard voice, his eyes resting briefly on Elle who stared back at him in shock. John Gatewick wasn't her father. And she hadn't been conceived in a test tube nor genetically engineered. Her entire life was a lie, it was true, but not the one she thought.

"Now I guess you have a decision to make," Gatewick continued, his gaze shifting back to Chen.

"Take the ampule and let her go, or take your chances against Dr. Radchenko who has his own score to settle with you." He jerked his head in Dimitri's direction.

"You? I don't even know you!" Chen spat. "What score could you possibly have to settle with me other than the fact that I'm a *Fallen*?"

"First of all, you've dared to put your hands on my mate. That alone is enough to earn you a death sentence. And secondly, you do know me, although I'm not surprised you don't remember. I'm sure you thought I'd burnt to a crisp centuries ago, if you ever thought of me at all. Oh, but I've thought of you. Every single minute of every single day for seven hundred years, *Jebe*." Dimitri's eyes narrowed to slits and a wild and dangerous look settled over his features. It was a look unlike anything she'd ever seen and she realized this was the man he hadn't wanted her to see, this was the venom he hadn't wanted her to know he was capable of. But now, faced with the man who had cost him everything, he was unable to keep it hidden any longer. And she was okay with it. As far as she was concerned, he had every right to feel as he did and the good he'd done in his long lifetime far outweighed his justifiable vendetta against this one evil monster. Elle felt Chen's whole body tremble against her. Clearly, Dimitri's words had jogged his memory.

"The farm boy? But…but that's impossible!"

Dimitri arched a dark brow. "Clearly not."

"So what will it be, Justin? Dr. Radchenko has given his word he won't lay a finger on you if you choose the vial and release the girl," Gatewick said, waving the item enticingly in the air.

"As if he can be taken at his word," Chen spat.

"I tire of this, John," Dimitri drawled, snatching the vial from the older man and tossing it in the air in Chen's direction. Keeping his fingers tangled in her hair, Chen released Elle's throat and lunged desperately for the prize. Taking advantage of the distraction, Elle dropped her hands, slipping free of the wig and diving for the floor. Dimitri's knife whistled through the air over her head, striking Chen with a deadly *thunk* and enough force to send him staggering backwards. The metallic clink of the vial hitting the floor and rolling out of his reach was immediately followed by the heavy thud of his body becoming close personal friends with the concrete.

Dimitri stalked across the lab and stood over Chen. For a moment, there was no sound but the heavy rasp of Chen's breathing as his lungs filled, slowly drowning him in his own blood.

"You gave your word you wouldn't touch me." Chen gurgled, then lapsed into a fit of moist coughing.

"And I didn't. But I never said I wouldn't kill you."

"Semantics," Chen wheezed. Then his eyes opened wide and he coughed one last time, spewing blood all over Dimitri's leather pants as though determined to have the last word, before death took him.

"Whatever." Dimitri bent to retrieve his stiletto, and after wiping it clean on the hem of Chen's jacket, he slapped it back into place against his forearm where it dissolved into his tattoo.

Rubbing his hands together until they glowed with an unearthly blue light, he turned his palms in the direction of Chen's body. Elle watched in awe as the remains of the *Fallen* simply vaporized and disappeared as though he had never been. But he had been, and what misery he'd inflicted on first Dimitri's family, she flicked a glance at John Gatewick who'd remained in the doorway watching her, and then on hers.

Dimitri completed his clean-up duty by working the same magic on the black puddle that had been the *animorti* and then scooped up her shoes. He turned just as Elle pulled herself up on shaking legs and dragged the skullcap from her head, freeing her hair with a sigh. He'd intended to give her a stern lecture about following directions. He'd intended to kick her ass for putting herself at risk. He'd intended to point out that by coming here she'd pretty much proven she had no faith in his ability to take care of himself. Instead, he looked at this woman, his woman, the woman who had put her life on the line and willingly swan dived into her own personal lake of fire to save him. Her clothes dripped with *animorti* guts, her pantyhose hung in tattered ruins, and her left eye was glued shut from the combination of make-up and tears. Frankly, she resembled a dog's breakfast. She'd never looked more beautiful to him. All the things he intended to say evaporated into thin air as she blinked up at him through her tangled hair and one bright, mascara caked eye.

"I told you those shoes were worth the money," she quipped while offering him a tentative smile.

He was across the room, pulling her into his arms, and settling his lips over hers before she'd even managed to draw another breath.

It was several minutes before Dimitri became aware the pounding he heard wasn't simply his own heart reacting to the woman in his arms. He opened one eye to see John Gatewick scurry across the lab and run up the stairs with more speed and agility than Dimitri would have expected from a man his age. When the sound of the door opening was followed by Gatewick's cry of alarm and the angry voices of Alec McAllister, Mac, and Galen, it belatedly occurred to Dimitri that they still believed Elle's uncle was her father and playing for the opposing team. He didn't have a real problem with letting them knock the guy around a little. After all, he'd put Elle through hell even if he'd thought it was for the right reasons. And he was human, so Dimitri knew the others wouldn't actually kill him. But Elle seemed to grasp the situation at the same moment and tore herself from his arms to limp to the foot of the stairs and call up to the others.

"It's okay! We're fine," she shouted over the din. "Let him go."

Heavy boots stomped down the stairs and Alec and Mac appeared, holding Gatewick by the arms between them, with Galen bringing up the rear. No one looked happy, least of all John Gatewick, who, when Dimitri considered it, had really had one hell of a day.

"He's cool," Dimitri confirmed, coming to stand behind Elle and wrapping his arms around her. "I'll explain everything later, but for now, put the guy down, huh?"

"Yeah?" McAllister arched a brow but looked to Elle for permission rather than Dimitri.

She looked into Gatewick's pale face for a minute before nodding decisively. "Yeah."

As soon as his hands were free, Alec stepped forward and grabbed Elle by the shoulders, giving her a little shake despite the growl that rumbled out of

Dimitri.

"You just stuff it for five," he snapped at the bigger man. "She scared a century off my life and if she wasn't your mate, I'd put her devious little butt right over my knee. The plan, Elle. Remember the plan? What happened to the freakin' plan?"

"I, um, changed the plan?" Elle squeaked.

"Do you have any idea what went through my mind when I couldn't reach you? Then an *animorti* walked in the door. We all know they never travel alone. I took care of him, put the receptionist out, and came looking for you. And do you know what I found? Do you?" Alec was shouting loud enough to shatter glass, yet Elle didn't as much as flinch. She simply rested her back against Dimitri and waited as the tirade wore one.

"I would imagine you found a vestibule with two locked doors and a faint trace of evil in the air," Elle replied quietly.

"Damn straight I did! What in the hell were you thinking?"

"I wasn't."

"What?" Alec stammered, letting his hands drop back to his sides at her honest admission.

"I said I wasn't thinking. I was feeling. I knew Dimitri was here as soon as the door opened and I was afraid to wait. I realize I should have at least let you know what I was doing, but frankly, I wasn't sure how. I'm sorry I worried you. But everything turned okay in the end, right?"

"That isn't the point, Elle, and you know it," Mac interjected. "You can't just twist situations in real life to suit yourself and count on controlling the outcome the way you do in a book. What if there'd been another *animorti* down here?"

"There was." Dimitri grinned over Elle's head. Oh sure, he'd give her a good talking to when they got home. Seeing her in Jebe's clutches had probably taken a century off of his life, too. But right at this moment, he couldn't help bursting with pride at her resourcefulness in taking down the *animorti*. "She killed it."

"She…how?" Mac's brows flew into his hairline and he nearly choked on his words.

Elle tipped her head back to grin at Dimitri. She may have winked but with one eye sealed tightly closed, he couldn't be sure. She looked back at the others and hefted her ruined shoes in the air with a grin.

"Jimmy Choo, not just for fashion anymore."

Epilogue

"What do you think?"

Dimitri surveyed the honey-colored hardwood floors running the length of the open space and the wall of windows allowing the bright afternoon sunlight to spill into every corner and simply shrugged. Elle twirled around happily in the center of the empty condo like a manic ballerina before skidding to a stop in front of him and wrapping her arms around his waist.

"Well?" she persisted.

"It's a little too uptown for my taste, but it's definitely got enough space and that's the whole idea, right?" He wrapped his arms around her and drew her closer, resting his chin on her head. Frankly, he thought the less space they had between them, the better.

"Well, yeah," she replied in a doubtful tone. "But if you don't like it, I could just as easily set up a desk in the corner of your studio and work from there."

"And have Jim-by-the-way traipsing in and out with notes and questions and worshipping you with his big puppy eyes a hundred times a day? No thanks." True to his word, Jim had remained in the cell exactly as Dimitri instructed until everything had been resolved. Once Dimitri was able to convince Elle the kid really was just an overzealous fan, and an aspiring romance author himself, she'd softened toward him and decided to try him out as her personal assistant and protégé. Dimitri was okay with that, but the unadulterated adoration with which the kid looked at Elle got on his last nerve after about five minutes. Dimitri had tried staring daggers and even occasionally growling at him, but like Elle, he appeared completely unintimidated by the leather-clad giant and nothing deterred him from his steadfast devotion, not even the reams of research Elle assigned him now that she'd decided to branch out into historical fiction. She'd concluded that between Dimitri's impressive library and the firsthand information she could tease out of him and the others, she'd be able to write the most painstakingly accurate historicals on the market.

"Jealous?" Elle propped her chin on his chest and looked up at him with a saucy grin.

"Hardly. I just prefer he worship you from afar. Or at least from a different room where I don't have to be subjected to it," Dimitri chuckled, dropping a kiss on her forehead. "So what do you think? You want this place or what?"

Elle blew out a long breath and her brows formed an inverted V.

"Well, the terrace seems awfully small. I know how much you enjoy the one you have now."

"True, but there's room for a couple of chairs and the park is right on our doorstep."

"We'll have to hire someone to build some bookcases. We do have more than a couple of books between the two of us, you know." Elle frowned, examining the long wall opposite the windows. "It's a shame the ones at your place are built-ins and we can't bring them along. They're gorgeous."

"Thanks, I always was good with my hands," he

waggled his brows suggestively and walked his fingers down her back to cup her buttocks through her jeans when she turned back to him with a look of astonishment.

"You *built* those?"

"Galen helped." He shrugged. "Much beer was consumed."

Elle shook her head. "I still feel like there's so much about you I don't know."

"You know the important stuff," Dimitri smiled. "The rest is just excess baggage acquired while trying to fill the emptiness of too many years alone."

"Hmmm. Well, I hope you won't be wishing for a little emptiness in a couple of decades when you find you're still stuck with me."

"Doubtful."

"Well, it certainly seems to have everything we need. Even if we used that entire wall for books, there's still plenty of wall space to display your paintings." She snagged her bottom lip between her teeth and looked around slowly before returning her gaze to his face. "I assume we won't be hanging your impressive portrait of a certain general?"

"So you've decided to abandon all attempts at subtlety?"

He'd had little to nothing to say about settling the grudge he'd been nursing for seven hundred years. Elle had been tossing out hints for weeks, trying to get him to open up.

"Subtlety is highly over-rated. Besides, it wasn't working. You finally found and killed the man who cost you your family, your friends, everything you loved and you haven't had two words to say about it. You must feel something? Whatever it is, it's okay. Don't you understand by now you can tell me anything? There's nothing that could ever diminish my opinion of you. It isn't good to keep things bottled up inside, Dimitri."

"Fine," he sighed, touching his forehead to hers and looking into her eyes. "You want to know why I haven't said anything? Basically, because I didn't have anything to say. You're right. I should feel something. I expected to feel something. Some sense of a weight being lifted from my shoulders, some sense of satisfaction. Something. But I didn't. I don't feel a damn thing. There's never any peace in killing, Elle, no matter how much someone deserves to die. Besides, his death doesn't really change anything, you know? It doesn't bring anyone back. Not my family, not yours. Not anyone."

"Really?" Elle's finely arched brows drew together in a frown. "Nothing at all?"

"Don't think so." He shrugged. She continued to regard him with a worried, skeptical expression. "Oh for the love of…all right, if you insist I have to feel something, maybe I *do* feel a little bit of relief knowing he won't be destroying any more lives. Yeah, maybe a little relief."

As he said the words, he realized it was true. Relief. It wasn't the profound, earth shattering emotion he expected to feel, but he'd finally gained justice for his family, for his losses. And he'd ensured that at least one *Fallen* could never inflict that same grief or terror on anyone again. Relief. He guessed it was something.

"Satisfied?"

"It's a start," she smiled, stretching up on her toes to plant a kiss on his jaw. He looped an arm around her waist and hauled her against him for a much longer and more satisfying kiss. Maybe revenge really was a dish best served cold. Or maybe, he thought as Elle melted against him, it had been so anticlimactic pulling his boots free of the bitter muck of the past because he now found it a lot easier to leave it behind and contemplate stepping into the future.

"So, do you want to make an offer on this place or do you want to keep looking?" He asked as he raised his head at last. "Mac and Katrina are expecting us for dinner and we're going to be late, so make up your mind."

"I don't know. You hate it, don't you?"

"I don't hate it," Dimitri replied mildly. "I just don't love it as much as you do."

"But it will be your home as much as mine, so I want it to be a place you love, too."

Dimitri tipped his head back, looked up at the fifteen-foot ceiling, and counted to ten. Then he dropped his chin to his chest, buried his fingers in Elle's hair on either side of her head, and cupped her face in his hands, tilting her face up to his.

"You still don't get it, do you?"

"Get what?" Elle crinkled her nose at him in that adorable way that made him lose his train of thought. In fact, just about every time she looked directly into his eyes it made him lose his train of thought, or at least diverted the train onto a completely different track. It was an ongoing problem, but one he found he didn't mind in the least.

"As long as you love it, I don't have to. I can, and have, lived just about anywhere and frankly, most of the places weren't nearly this appealing. If you asked to me to live in a refrigerator box under the Brooklyn Bridge, I'd be on board as long as you were right there in that box with me. Four walls don't make a place home, people do. I haven't had a real home in centuries, but I do now. I can live anywhere, Arabella Penelope Gatewick, as long as it's with you."

"Oh," she sighed into his mouth as his lips covered hers again.

****

By the time they faded into the hallway outside the McAllister's penthouse an hour and a half later, they'd not only put in an offer on the condo, they'd christened nearly every room in the place.

Elle pressed the bell, leaned back against Dimitri, and wondered for the thousandth time what she'd ever done to deserve such happiness. The feeling of complete and utter bliss lasted right up until the moment the door opened and she found herself looking into the big, blue eyes of Callista McAllister, the woman she'd buried alive in the catacombs of Rome.

"Elle!" Callista twisted her thick braid nervously, then smiled warmly and opened her arms. "We thought you'd never get here. I've been dying to see you."

Elle leaned away from the intended embrace and burrowed further into Dimitri.

"Is that supposed to be some kind of double entendre? You don't have to remind me I tried to kill you, Callista. Believe me, no one knows it better than I do."

"You said they'd gone back to Rome. You lied to me, you stinking bastard."

"You needed to face her sooner or later."

"Later would have been my preference had you

bothered to ask."

"Which is why I didn't.

"If my uncle is in there too, you are toast, Sir!"

"No, he really did go to Switzerland with Michael and Alec to retrieve the contents of the ampule. You're off the hook with him for the moment."

Dimitri's loving laughter invaded and wrapped around her mind. And then the big lug shoved her right into Callista McAllister. As the other woman's arms came around her, Elle forgot to breathe. And when she finally sucked in a breath, it caught on a sob. Before she knew it, she was bawling like a reformed sinner at a revival meeting.

"I'm so s-s-sorry, Calli. I would never hurt you intentionally. N-n-never."

Calli gripped Elle by her shaking shoulders and pulled away, looking directly and earnestly into her eyes. "Please believe me that it never even entered my mind that you would. We all know that wasn't you. Let's face it, Elle, it's a pretty good bet if you came to Rome in your right mind, you wouldn't be caught dead in some dusty old catacomb. You'd have headed straight for Via Condotti." Calli laughed, referring to one of the most exclusive and expensive shopping streets in Rome.

"Good point," Elle sniffed, dabbing at her eyes with the cuff of her sweater. "You've actually forgiven me, haven't you?"

"There was never anything to forgive. Look at me! I'm fine. I'm happy, I'm madly in love, and…" Calli glanced around at Luca who reclined in an armchair with one long leg slung casually over the other watching his wife like a cat watches a canary. Calli gasped as though the mere sight of him still took her breath away, then looked back at Elle with a brilliant smile and a becoming flush staining her cheeks. "And I'm having a baby."

"You're...oh gosh! That's wonderful!" Elle simply stared, dumbfounded, until Dimitri leaned around her to kiss Calli on the cheek.

"Congratulations, kid." Callista stepped back and Dimitri gently shoved Elle through the door and closed it behind them. Luca rose to his feet and offered his hand to Dimitri who yanked him forward to pound him on the back.

"Congratulations, brother."

"Thanks."

Stepping back, Luca grabbed Calli's hand before turning his attention to Elle.

"You're looking well. I was worried. Well...anyway, I'm glad you're okay," he mumbled before dropping his gaze.

"Of course, I'm okay," Elle said glancing between Luca and Calli with a puzzled frown. "Why wouldn't I be okay?"

Calli piped up when Luca remained silent. "Luca has been a bit worried there might be lasting damage. You know...from his dagger in your chest."

"Seriously?" Elle's jaw nearly hit the floor as she turned wide eyes in Luca's direction. "You were worried about *me*? You would have been well within your rights to kill me outright if that's what it took to stop Azakriel, Luca."

Luca glanced up slyly from beneath his lashes. "So you agree it was the demon who was responsible for everything?"

"Of course it was the demon! I know you never would have tried to kill me, otherwise," Elle agreed emphatically.

"And you never would have buried Callista in the catacombs otherwise," he announced in a tone of finality. "Now can we eat? You're late and I'm starving."

"You're always starving," Calli laughed, dragging her husband toward the table.

"You tricked me. You all tricked me."

"Yep." Elle detected the satisfied amusement in Dimitri's voice as his arms came around her from behind.

"Thank you," she sighed happily, leaning back into him and drawing on his strength. The strength he never failed to offer and she'd come to easily depend upon.

"My pleasure."

"Is it safe to come in, yet?" Kassian McAllister called from the kitchen.

"Depends," Elle called back. "Do you have clothes on this time?"

"Oh for heaven's sake, Kassian," Kat grumbled as she shouldered past him in the doorway carrying a platter of balsamic chicken which she set on the dining room table. She turned to Elle with a bright smile. "Did Calli tell you I'm going to be an auntie?"

"Yes." Elle grinned back and stepped forward to hug her friend. "It's wonderful news."

"We have some news, too," Dimitri offered, pulling out a chair for Elle before dropping into the one next to her. "We finally put an offer in on a place."

"That's great," McAllister said. "Took you long enough to find one you liked."

"Well, Elle loves it, and it's got plenty of room, three baths, five bedrooms, so I figured, what the hell. It's only money, right?" He laced his fingers through hers and squeezed.

"Five bedrooms? What exactly do you need five bedrooms for?"

"Well, of course five bedrooms," Elle held up her free hand and ticked them off on her fingers. "One for us, naturally. One for Dimitri's studio, one for my office, and one for guests. I mean, when he gets back from Switzerland, I might want to invite my...uncle for a visit. Eventually."

"So you've forgiven him?" Kat asked, plunking down a wicker basket filled with warm bread and slapping Luca's hand as it snaked forward to snag a piece of chicken before they were all seated.

"Not entirely, but I'm sure I'll come around at some point. I mean, I definitely don't agree with the way he handled things, but..."

"But baby, even if the way he handled it was wrong, it was for the right reasons. He made some poor choices and found himself in an impossible situation. Everything he did from that point on was motivated by love and a desire to protect you," Dimitri added, releasing her fingers and wrapping an arm around her shoulders to pull her closer instead. "He's an old man, and you're all the family he has left."

"I know and I keep reminding myself of that, but the hurt ran so deep for so long it's tough to just pretend it never happened. But you're right, and I'm sure I'll get past it eventually. Besides, he's the only one who can tell me about my parents," Elle added wistfully turning to Kat. "My mother really did love the scent of

231

lilacs."

"Of course she did," Kat smiled, dropping into a chair next to her husband.

"Okay, so back to this place you found. That's only four. Why do you need a fifth bedroom?" McAllister frowned as Dimitri rolled his eyes and looked away.

"Isn't it obvious, my love?" Kat asked. "After all, this is *Elle* we're talking about."

Kat glanced at Elle, Elle winked at Calli. Then all three looked expectantly at McAllister while he thought it through.

"By the Saints," he chuckled at last. "Dimitri, my brother, you own one pair of sneakers and two pair of motorcycle boots. It must really be love if you're laying out dough for a five bedroom on the Upper East Side so Elle has a room for her..." He broke off choking as a fit of laughter took him.

"Shoes!" the three women cried in unison.

A word about the author...

Sharon Saracino was born and raised in the beautiful anthracite coal region of Northeastern Pennsylvania. A lifelong love of writing took a back seat to real life while she got married, raised a family, went back to college, and finally decided what she wanted to be when she grew up! The oldest of three siblings, she was raised in a small town rich in history and filled with characters galore!

Sharon is a member of Pennwriters, Romance Writers of America, the Fantasy, Futuristic and Paranormal Chapter, and the Maryland Romance Writers.

When she is not reading, writing, or dabbling in photography and genealogy, she works full time as a Certified Registered Rehabilitation Nurse. She plans to win the lottery just as soon as she remembers to buy a ticket, fantasizes about moving to Italy, brews limoncello, and spends time with her incredible husband, funny and talented son, and two crazy dogs.

http://sharonsaracino.com